"You can't just ignore me, Sebastián."

Of course he could. He could do anything he wanted. He was a duke. Still, he was simply being petty now and more than that, trying to put off the inevitable moment when he'd have to stop and look into her dark eyes. Feel that same kick of desire deep inside him, the same tug of recognition. Knowing that this time there was nothing to stop him from taking what he wanted. What they both wanted...

But that was impossible. Edward and Emily might be gone, he might be a widower and Alice a widow, but there was too much between them now. Too many promises he'd made that he couldn't put aside for the sake of mere sex.

Except that made no difference to the punch of emotion that hit him the moment her gaze met his, the restless, aching want that pulled at him.

Jackie Ashenden writes dark, emotional stories with alpha heroes who've just gotten the world to their liking only to have it blown apart by their kick-ass heroines. She lives in Auckland, New Zealand, with her husband, the inimitable Dr. Jax, two kids and two rats. When she's not torturing alpha males and their gutsy heroines, she can be found drinking chocolate martinis, reading anything she can lay her hands on, wasting time on social media or being forced to go mountain biking with her husband. To keep up-to-date with Jackie's new releases and other news, sign up to her newsletter at jackieashenden.com.

Books by Jackie Ashenden

Harlequin Presents

The Innocent's One-Night Proposal
The Maid the Greek Married
His Innocent Unwrapped in Iceland
A Vow to Redeem the Greek

Rival Billionaire Tycoons

A Diamond for My Forbidden Bride
Stolen for My Spanish Scandal

Three Ruthless Kings

Wed for Their Royal Heir
Her Vow to Be His Desert Queen
Pregnant with Her Royal Boss's Baby

The Teras Wedding Challenge

Enemies at the Greek Altar

Visit the Author Profile page
at Harlequin.com for more titles.

Spanish Marriage Solution

JACKIE ASHENDEN

PRESENTS

HARLEQUIN®
PRESENTS™

Recycling programs
for this product may
not exist in your area.

ISBN-13: 978-1-335-59361-0

Spanish Marriage Solution

Copyright © 2024 by Jackie Ashenden

For questions and comments about the quality of this book,
please contact us at CustomerService@Harlequin.com.

TM and ® are trademarks of Harlequin Enterprises ULC.

Harlequin Enterprises ULC
22 Adelaide St. West, 41st Floor
Toronto, Ontario M5H 4E3, Canada
www.Harlequin.com

Printed in Lithuania

MIX
Paper | Supporting
responsible forestry
FSC® C021394

Spanish Marriage
Solution

To Ajax, king of scourers!

CHAPTER ONE

ALICE SMITH COULD pinpoint the exact second her life was ruined.

It was the moment she met her brother-in-law.

Five years later and nothing had changed.

Sebastián Castellano, Tenth Duke of Aveira, was still as mesmerisingly beautiful as he had been when Emily had first brought him back to Auckland to show her new husband off to the family. And even now, after all those years and with Emily only two months dead, Alice still felt the same gut punch that she'd always felt every time she was in his presence.

The last time she'd seen him had been at Emily's funeral, in Auckland, and he'd flown all the way from Spain to attend. He hadn't spoken to Alice. He hadn't spoken at all. He'd sat in the back of the church and by the time everyone had filed past the casket and placed on top of it the sprigs of fern frond that Alice had organised, he'd gone.

He'd barely been in the country a day.

Alice's husband Edward's funeral had been the day after, but Alice hadn't been expecting Sebastián to attend that. Why would he? The whole reason Emily and Edward were dead was because they'd both been in the same car that had plunged off the side of a mountain in Switzerland.

Turned out that Emily hadn't been having some 'me time' in Greece as she'd told everyone. She'd been in Switzerland, having an affair with Edward.

Not that the affair was relevant now. The only thing that mattered, or at least the only thing that mattered to Alice, was Diego, Emily's four-month-old son.

Who was not, as it turned out, Sebastián's.

No, he was Edward's. Edward and her sister's, and he was why she was here in Seville, after a nightmare forty-eight-hour journey from Auckland, involving three plane changes and an excruciatingly expensive taxi to the Castellano family's estate, a hacienda, nestled at the base of some rather impressive mountains.

She felt slightly sick with jet lag and the hot, dusty air didn't help, but she took a fortifying breath and shaded her eyes from the intense heat of the midday Spanish sun. She was sweating in the dark suit she'd foolishly decided to wear for the trip and the nerves that had got worse and worse the closer she came to the Castellano estate were now wreaking havoc in her gut.

Sebastián was a difficult man and confronting him wasn't going to be easy, especially about this. But it had to be done. Her nephew was more important to her than anything and she was here to bring him home, back to New Zealand where he belonged.

Ahead of her was the large wooden corral she remembered from previous trips to the Castellano hacienda. The Castellanos had been breeding Andalusian horses for centuries and were currently the lead supplier of Andalusians in the world. Their bloodlines were highly sought after, used for dressage, showjumping and other competitions, and Sebastián was a world-renowned talent as a breeder and trainer.

Alice had always loved visiting the stables whenever she'd come to Spain, which had been every Christmas after Emily had married Sebastián. He'd covered travel expenses for the Smiths and her and Emily's parents while they'd been alive, which had been very generous of him. However, the only part of those visits that Alice had enjoyed was seeing the horses. She'd been a horse girl once when she'd been small, and a part of her still thrilled at the sight the magnificent animals. Emily, on the other hand, had been afraid of them.

Emily certainly wouldn't have liked the magnificent, glossy black stallion currently trotting around the perimeter of the corral on a lead rope. The rope was held by a figure standing in the middle of the dusty corral circle, watching as the horse paced around him.

He was exceptionally tall, dwarfing even Alice, who was five nine in her bare feet, his shoulders wide and muscular. He had the long, lean shape of an athlete, the plain black T-shirt and dusty jeans he wore only emphasising his magnificent physique.

His raven-black hair was as glossy as the horse's

coat and even though his face was slightly turned away from her, she didn't need to see it to remember him. That face haunted her dreams. The precisely carved features of an aristocrat: high cheekbones, straight nose, and a firm hard mouth. Eyes of dark, smoky gold.

She hadn't told him she was coming. She hadn't wanted him to know why she was here, not until they were face to face. This wasn't the kind of conversation you could have over the phone, and especially not with him. Emily's letter was in her handbag, creased and stained with tears, but Alice needed to show it to him. It was proof of what her sister had wanted in case she ended up having a fight on her hands. She hoped not. She hoped that Sebastián, scion of an ancient dukedom whose history and business dealt in ancient bloodlines, wouldn't want to bring up the child of an affair his wife had had with another man.

He was proud, so Emily had often said, and proud of his family line, so Alice couldn't imagine him welcoming Diego. Perhaps he'd even be glad she was here to take the child off his hands.

When she'd arrived, Lucia, the housekeeper who managed the huge white stucco hacienda that was the Castellano estate, had greeted her like a long-lost daughter and had told her that 'Señor Sebastián' was in the stables looking over a new purchase. Lucia had tried to get Alice to sit down and have something cooling to drink, but Alice had insisted on seeing Sebastián immediately. She wanted to get this over and done with as soon as possible, so Lucia had got Tomas, the stable manager, to bring her to Sebastián.

Which was why she was now standing here in the baking sun, watching said 'new purchase', the beautiful horse, come to a stop directly in front of Sebastián. He pulled something out of his pocket, an apple, and held it out in his palm. The stallion dropped his head, soft mouth closing around the fruit, eating it directly from Sebastián's hand.

It was oddly mesmerising to watching Sebastián reach out and stroke the horse's soft nose. He had a magic touch with the animals, Emily had once told her, pulling a face as she did so. In fact, he'd seemed to like the horses more than he did her, which was a regular complaint from Emily. Alice hadn't taken any notice, which in retrospect had been a mistake. She'd thought it was Emily being dramatic and annoyed at not having attention twenty-four-seven, but apparently it hadn't been.

The stable manager opened the corral gate and went in, going over to where Sebastián stood. There was a brief conversation in rapid Spanish before Sebastián's head turned sharply in Alice's direction.

And as it always did whenever he looked at her, all the air escaped her lungs, and her heart began to race.

It happened every single time.

She hated it.

She'd first met him five years earlier, after his and Emily's whirlwind wedding. They'd come out to New Zealand to meet the in-laws, and it had happened then too, as they'd stood awkwardly on her parents' deck overlooking Waitemata Harbour. The moment his golden eyes had met hers, she'd felt an almost visceral impact. The gut punch of fierce physical attraction, and more than that, for her at least. She hadn't been able to put into words the nature of the emotion that had coursed through her, only that somehow a fire in her had responded to a fire in him, recognising a kindred spirit.

She had no idea why. She didn't know him, had never met him before that day. It was just something about him that had reached inside her and closed its fingers around her heart. But she'd been married to Edward and he'd just married Emily and so there had been nothing to be done about it.

She'd put the feeling behind her, ignored it. Buried it so far down inside her that she could pretend it had never been there in the first place. Easy enough when he and Emily had lived in Andalusia, in the ancient Castellano hacienda. Alice and Edward had seen them only once a year at Christmas.

Alice had become adept at hiding her feelings. At never letting even a hint of what she felt for him show. Yet every time she was anywhere near him, she'd feel that same gut punch, that pull, like a magnet drawing her to him. And perhaps the worst thing about it was that there had been times when she'd catch his eye, and she'd see something glowing in the depths, something that made her think that he felt the same way. But she'd ignored that too, since, even if he did feel the same way, they had both been married.

Out in the corral, Sebastián looked away from her, said something to Tomas and turned his attention back to the horse.

Tomas walked back out of the corral, shutting the gate behind him and coming over to where Alice stood. She was getting sticky with sweat, her suit rumpled and far too constricting.

'Señora Smith,' Tomas said in heavily accented English. He must be new, because she didn't know him and she'd got to know most of Sebastián's employees over the years. 'Su Excelencia is busy. But you may wait in the hacienda until he is able to speak with you.'

A thread of anger wound through her. She was hot, sweaty, and jet-lagged and the longer she waited to talk to him about Diego, the harder it was going to be. Because of course nothing about having to deal with Sebastián was ever easy.

It wasn't that she didn't talk to him. She did. But only when it was impossible to do otherwise, and even then their conversations were short, stilted, and awkward. He was polite to her, but cold and distant, so she tried to avoid him when she could, and when she couldn't, she treated him with icy formality. For a while she'd even entertained the hope that Emily might not notice that her sister and her husband didn't get on.

A false hope.

Emily had soon decided that since it was clear Alice

and Sebastián didn't like each other, they needed to be forced into proximity so they could learn to 'get along'.

It had been excruciating and eventually Alice had had to tell Emily to stop. Yes, maybe they didn't much like each other, but they were adults and could handle a bit of dislike without burning things to the ground.

Emily didn't need to know that for Alice the opposite was true.

Alice stared at the tall figure in the corral, but he didn't look back again.

Did he know why she was here? Was that why he'd ordered her to wait in the hacienda? Had Emily told him that Diego wasn't his? Had he known that she was having an affair with Edward before the car accident? Had it been as much of a shock to him as it had to her?

She really should do what he'd said and go back inside the hacienda to wait. She was hot and tired, and it would be better to have this discussion in the cool of the house.

Then again, since she'd started her investment company, she'd become unaccustomed to waiting for men to speak first. Being proactive and taking charge before they even knew they were dealing with a woman was always the best approach. Never let it enter their heads that she was female. That way, by the time they realised who they were talking with, it was too late.

Being female in the world of finance was problematic to say the least. Then again, she'd spent a lot of time trying hard not to be female, which would make dealing with Sebastián a lot less of a problem.

She'd had years of practice at hiding the way she felt about him, at hiding her own feelings, full stop, and that was how she'd go about negotiating this particular situation. She'd tell him logically, calmly, that Emily had sent her a letter about Diego, and that her sister wanted Alice to bring him up should anything happen to her. That was why she was here. To take her nephew back home to New Zealand where he belonged.

And there was nothing Sebastián could do about it. End of story.

Sebastián tried to focus on Halcón, the stallion, but it was difficult.

He could still feel the hard shock of Alice's unexpected presence echoing through him, and it was proving complicated to get control of himself. Much harder than it should have been, especially after all the years of practice.

He'd learned the art of control early, since his father wouldn't stand for anything less than total self-mastery, and it had come in useful when all his plans, all his dreams for the future, had come crashing down following Emily's death. Then again, he was used to life's body blows.

Meeting Alice for the first time had been one of them.

He hadn't known who she was right away. She'd

been standing on the deck at Emily's parents' house, with the views out over the blue water, smiling at something Emily's father had said. Her hair had tumbled over her shoulders in glossy waves, black as a raven's wing, and while her features didn't have Emily's petite, precise beauty, there was something about their arrangement that caught his attention. A strong face, animated and expressive. Not typically beautiful but captivating all the same. Winged black eyebrows, a strong, decisive nose, and a long, sensual mouth. She had skin the colour of dark honey, and when her deep brown eyes had met his, he'd felt a tectonic shift inside him. As if the earth had moved on its axis, changing gravity, changing the seasons, changing the very air he breathed.

Then Emily had introduced them and he'd understood, without a shadow of a doubt, that the worst had happened: he'd married the wrong sister.

Halcón dropped his head and nudged at Sebastián's hand, questing for another treat, but Sebastián wasn't paying attention. He didn't need to turn around to know that Alice hadn't gone back into the hacienda as he'd told her to, and he could feel her watching him, the way he'd always been able to feel it. Even now it still had the power to steal his breath, the way it had done for the past five years.

But he'd made a vow to himself, the day he'd met her, that he'd ignore the change to his life's axis. That he wouldn't let mere physical attraction—because surely that was all it was—affect him in any way.

It was meaningless. She was meaningless. She was his sister-in-law and that was all. He'd already married the woman he intended to spend his life with. He'd made vows to her, promises he'd keep until his dying breath. The Dukes of Aveira the Castellanos, as his father had often told him, had honour in their blood, and, because he was not truly a Castellano, he must learn how to be honourable. And he had learned. It wasn't a lesson he'd ever forget.

So when he heard her say his name, in the low, husky voice that seemed to stroke over his skin and take hold of something inside him, he didn't turn immediately. He directed his attention to the horse, gripping the lead rein and stepping in close.

'Sebastián,' Alice said again. 'I need to talk to you. It's important.'

Of course it would be important. She hadn't flown all the way from New Zealand to arrive unannounced at the Castellano hacienda for nothing, and he suspected he knew the reason she was here. Diego. There wouldn't be anything else that would bring her half-way around the world to his doorstep.

Not even you?

Before he'd met Emily, he'd had many lovers. He was experienced with women. He knew when a woman wanted him, and Alice had wanted him. He'd seen the flare in her dark eyes the moment their gazes had connected. That had made it imperative that he never let slip his own feelings and, so far, he never had.

So no, she wouldn't be here for him, but even if she were, he wouldn't do anything about it. The fact that their spouses had been cheating with each other only made his own determination not to even stronger.

'As I told Tomas, I'm busy,' he said curtly. 'Go into the hacienda. Lucia will give you coffee. I'll be another half-hour.' Without waiting for a response, he gripped Halcón's mane and pulled himself up onto the stallion's back with the casual ease of long practice.

Halcón shifted beneath him, dancing sideways as Sebastián's weight settled.

You know why she's here and yet you think the horse is more important?

Oh, the horse was important. New blood for the stables that were descended from the warhorses of old, that the ancient dukes had once ridden into battle on. But nothing was more important than Diego. His son. And he *was* Sebastián's son, no matter what the DNA tests said. He'd been with Emily when she'd given birth and he'd been the first to hold him. The first to look down into his face, and he'd felt the same shift then that he'd felt when he'd met Alice, as if nothing would ever be the same again.

He hadn't thought Alice would know the secret of Diego's parentage, but somehow she'd found out, and while her visit wasn't entirely unexpected, it definitely wasn't welcome. He needed time. Time to decide what he was going to do about it, about her, and he *was* going to do something. Nobody was taking Diego from him. Nobody.

Sebastián controlled the stallion effortlessly with his knees and laid a hand on the side of the animal's neck. Halcón settled, but Sebastián could still feel the tension in the horse's massive body. A spirited beast, which was good. He liked it when a horse had fire. Not so he could break it—to break an animal's spirit was a tragedy—but to channel it, enhance it.

'I don't want coffee,' Alice said. 'I need to talk to you. Now.'

There was a note of cool authority in her voice, very different from the warmth that had once infused every word. He'd noticed that the warmth had vanished not long after she'd set up her investment company, the same time he'd noticed that the passionate spark that had drawn him so intensely the day they'd met had died. He hadn't wanted to notice, of course, but he had all the same. Some inner light in her had been extinguished and she'd become cool and hard all over, like a field of golden sunflowers slowly being covered with ice.

He didn't know what had happened and he hadn't asked. He never spoke of her with Emily and Emily had learned by then never to bring up the subject of her sister.

Grief and regret twisted in his heart at the thought of his wife, as it had been doing since she'd died, but he thrust away both emotions. He'd failed Emily and he knew it, but he would not fail Diego. Not ever.

Ignoring Alice, he urged the horse into a trot around the corral, assessing its pace. Eventually she would get tired of waiting and do what he'd said. After all, it was hot out here and she must be jet-lagged.

Except she didn't leave.

She stood outside the corral and leaned over the fence posts, watching him. Making it very obvious that she wasn't going to move.

Emily had never come to the stables. She'd been afraid of the horses, which should have been a red flag, but he'd refused to see it. She had been petite and delicate, and even though she'd acted more fragile than she actually was, he'd enjoyed being cast in the role of her protector. That was what he'd been born for, to protect, like the dukes of old.

But Alice had never been afraid of the horses. Every time she and Edward had visited, she'd come to the stables at some point and watch his stable hands. It had been distracting. Eventually he'd had to tell her, curtly, that the stables were out of bounds to visitors.

It seemed she hadn't remembered that fact.

'I can stand here all day,' Alice said as he trotted past her for the second time. 'You can't just ignore me, Sebastián.'

Of course he could. He could do anything he wanted. He was a duke. Still, he was simply being petty now and, more than that, trying to put off the inevitable moment when he'd have to stop and look into her dark eyes. Feel that same kick of desire deep inside him, the same tug of recognition. Knowing that this time there was nothing to stop him from taking what he wanted. What they both wanted…

But that was impossible. Edward and Emily might be gone, he might be a widower and Alice a widow, but there was too much between them now. Too many promises he'd made that he couldn't put aside for the sake of mere sex.

Avoiding her was cowardice and he was not a coward.

After the second circuit, he finally drew Halcón up in front of her. He didn't dismount, instead looking down at her where she stood just outside the corral fence, dressed in a rumpled black suit and fitted white shirt. Her wealth of glossy black hair had been contained in a severe ponytail, not a wisp out of place, and it left her face looking naked. There were dark circles under her eyes, new lines of grief around her mouth.

He couldn't forget that while he'd lost his wife, Edward had meant nothing to him. Yet Alice had lost, not only her husband, but also her sister.

Except that made no difference to the punch of emotion that hit him the moment her gaze met his, the restless, aching want that pulled at him.

There were reasons he didn't speak to her. Reasons he tried never to be in the same room as her, and he'd thought he'd managed to kill the want over the years, but it had never got any easier.

It wasn't easy now, yet he managed to force away the familiar surge of need, steeling himself to meet her level gaze.

Despite her obvious weariness, she didn't seem to have any problems with looking at him, so perhaps she didn't feel it any more. He hoped so. It would make this a lot less complicated.

'I didn't think half an hour was too much to ask,' he said coolly. 'You'd be more comfortable inside.'

'Probably.' There was a determined cast to her chin now and she lifted it, as if he'd challenged her. 'But this can't wait.'

Halcón shifted again, as if picking up on his disquiet, but he put his hand on the horse's neck once more and the stallion settled. He stared at Alice, recognising abruptly something he hadn't seen in her in far too long—a spark.

It was bright, burning and fierce. But, as he already knew, it wasn't for him.

'You're here for Diego.' He didn't make it a question and there wasn't much point pussyfooting around the subject.

Her eyes widened, a ripple of surprise crossing her face. 'How did you—?'

'There's no other reason for you to be here, Alice.'

Slowly, she pushed herself away from the corral fence and straightened, the expression on her face almost imperious. 'No,' she said. 'No, you're right. There *is* no other reason for me to be here.'

He could feel the layers to that statement, but it wasn't worth trying to read deeper into what she was saying. He wouldn't be doing anything about it now, that was for certain, and he wasn't interested in doing so anyway.

'So what?' he demanded. 'What about Diego?'

Her dark eyes met his head-on. 'Emily's lawyers sent me a letter. He's not your son, Sebastián. She wanted me to look after him. So that's why I'm here. I'm here to take him home.'

CHAPTER TWO

ALICE'S PALMS WERE now damp and it wasn't only due to delivering a truth to Sebastián that he didn't want to hear. It was also him.

Watching him pull himself effortlessly up onto the horse's back and then ride without either saddle or reins, as if he and the horse were one beast, one mind, was like drinking a slug of whiskey straight down. It stole her breath then made her feel warm all over, and slightly intoxicated, a little drunk on his competence and the athleticism with which he performed every movement.

She'd seen him ride before, at other visits, and it had always been mesmerising. She didn't know anything about riding, but he seemed a natural to her, and it was clear the horses loved him too. They were always following him around and nuzzling at his pockets for treats, nickering at him and pushing at him with their long muzzles. He was so gentle with them, too. Not at all the cold, proud, arrogant man he was around everyone else, and that had fascinated her. Made her want to know why he was so different around animals. She'd wanted to ask Emily, but talking about him to Emily had felt too dangerous, so she hadn't. Going to the stables had felt dangerous too, and really, it would have been better for her peace of mind not to. Yet she hadn't been able to help herself. She was drawn helplessly there, by her fascination with the horses and with him.

She hadn't known her visits were a problem until he'd told her curtly that the stables were out of bounds to non-employees, and she was disturbing the horses.

It was a good thing, she'd told herself then, ignoring the hurt she'd felt at the time, because she had no right to feel that hurt. Of course, he didn't want her in the stables, especially if her presence disturbed the animals. She didn't work for him, so there was no reason for her to be there after all.

Yet still, watching him now, she felt that same combination of fascination and hurt that she'd felt years ago. The same combination of breathless desire and guilt. Nothing had changed.

God, how she hated it.

He sat on the back of the huge black stallion, his muscular body shifting with the horse's restless movements, automatically adjusting without any seeming effort. His gaze was hard, his smoky gold eyes as cold as she'd ever seen them, so it took her a second to register that he didn't look shocked in the least.

'What?' His voice was deep and dark, his lightly accented English making music of the words. 'You think I didn't know? You think I wasn't aware of Emily's affair? I had the tests done, Alice. So yes, I know he's not my son, not by blood. But he is in every other way that counts and so he's not going anywhere.'

She'd expected to shock him, because she certainly hadn't been aware of Edward's affair with Emily. Oh, she'd suspected that Edward might have been having an affair given his many absences overseas on 'business' trips and the emotional distance growing between them, but not that his affair had been with her sister. Not until the pair of them had died together in that car accident.

She hadn't expected that, not only had Sebastián known about the affair, but he'd also known that Diego wasn't his.

She felt as if the ground had been ripped from under her.

'How?' she asked blankly. 'How did you know?'

He lifted one powerful shoulder. 'That's not important. What is important is that my name is on Diego's birth certificate. I *am* his father.'

Alice felt the world shift again, like the horse between Sebastián's powerful thighs, and her gut churned. Jet lag of course, but also a shock she wasn't expecting to feel to add to the complicated tangle of emotions seeing him had brought back.

She'd thought he wouldn't argue. The Castellanos were an old-world, aristocratic family where blood was everything, and she'd assumed that Sebastián wouldn't want anything to do with a child not of his blood. That, after a period of surprise and anger, he'd have no issue with giving up a child that wasn't his and he wasn't responsible for.

With a supreme effort of will, Alice forced her shock and all the rest of her emotions away and met his steady, hard gaze. 'I don't care,' she said flatly. 'He's my nephew. I have a letter from Emily saying that she wanted me to bring him up and so that's what I'm going to do.' He was all she had left of Emily, all she'd ever have of a family of her own too, but she wasn't going to tell Sebastián that. He didn't know about her terrible miscarriage, but he did know that Diego was all she had left of her sister.

'I sympathise,' Sebastián said, his voice entirely without sympathy. 'Nevertheless, his place is here with me.'

Alice blinked, her nausea still churning, but she'd be damned if she looked weak and sick in front of him, so she reached for the anger instead. The anger that had been burning in her for months now, an anger she'd forced aside because her sister and her husband were dead and being angry with them wouldn't bring them back or change things. Except it might help her now.

She drew herself up to her full height, the way she did at work when men were trying to tell her how things worked. When they were trying to explain the world of finance to her, despite the fact that she knew it far better than they ever could.

'No,' she said icily. 'His place is with me. His aunt. By blood.' She held Sebastián's proud golden stare.

'If I have to get lawyers involved, believe me, I have no problem with that.'

The stallion shifted restlessly and Sebastián once again dropped a hand to absently stroke its glossy black coat. And despite herself, despite everything, Alice found her gaze drawn to that large, strong hand. White scars dotted the olive skin of his long fingers, evidence of a man who worked hard in an intensely physical job, no matter the wealth and power of his position.

She'd tried never to fantasise about him. Tried never to imagine that hand on her skin, stroking her as he stroked that horse, because she'd been married and she'd loved her husband. But sometimes, especially in the years after she'd lost the baby, before Edward had pulled away from her so completely, she'd found herself dreaming of Sebastián's hands on her body, and that hard mouth on hers. She'd always wake up with an aching sense of loss and suffocating guilt.

She still felt that guilt, another thread of pain to add to her grief at losing Emily, even though her sister had been having an affair with her husband. It was just all so complicated and fraught that she had no idea why she would even be looking at Sebastián's hand when she had so many other things to deal with. And even if the situation had been different, she had no idea what Sebastián felt about her. She never had. Nothing, judging from the expression on his arrogant face. It was clear that he wasn't going to give an inch.

'Do that,' he said. 'I also have lawyers. And they have been protecting Castellano interests for centuries. Diego is mine, Alice. And I keep what is mine.'

'Like you kept Emily?' It was a stupid thing to say, and she knew it as soon as the words were out of her mouth. She'd let her anger get the better of her, and that had never been a good thing. If he was going to be difficult about Diego then she needed to get him on her side, not the opposite.

His handsome features hardened even further. 'There is nothing for you here, Alice. Go home.' Then, before she could say anything else, he turned the horse away and set off on another circuit, urging the stallion into an easy canter.

Alice's heart thumped loudly in her ears, sweat trickling down her back, and, much to her horror, she felt tears prickling the backs of her eyes. She must be more tired than she'd thought if she was letting her emotions get to her like this.

Gritting her teeth, she blinked the tears away.

Tears were Emily's trick and one her sister had used often to get her way. Acting weak and fragile, looking like a victim to get attention. It had always worked, too, but Alice had learned early on that it was impossible trying to compete with her beautiful, feminine sister, and so she hadn't.

Instead she'd kept her emotions locked down, hidden away, becoming stoic and staunchly practical. And what had been a cause of pain in childhood became an asset in the corporate world. No one could ever accuse Alice Smith of being overly emotional.

She stood there a moment, getting herself under control.

She'd given herself a week in Spain, thinking that bringing Diego home would be a simple matter, and she still had time. Her lawyer threat hadn't been an idle one—there were some she could call on—but she knew that if Sebastián chose to be difficult about this, then fighting him was going to be hard. She didn't have the resources he did, plus she was unfamiliar with the Spanish legal system. Still, she'd be damned if she went home like a good little dog with her tail between her legs.

She'd already lost one child. She wasn't going to lose another.

He expected her to leave, which meant her only response was to stay. She certainly wasn't going to go without at least seeing her nephew and surely Sebastián couldn't deny her that. Perhaps, if she stayed a couple of days, she might even be able to convince him to change his mind about her taking Diego back to New Zealand.

He is not going to change his mind. He's not going to give that child up and you know it.

Alice took a silent, steadying breath, gazing at Sebastián as he rode another circuit.

Emily hadn't confided much of her marital issues to Alice—now Alice knew about Edward, she could see why—but she had told her that Sebastián could be arrogant and cold, and that he was exceptionally strong-willed. Difficult, Emily had once said, but since he was also amazing in bed—something Alice really didn't want to know—she forgave him his difficulties.

Well, Alice had caught a glimpse of that arrogance and coldness just now, also a ruthlessness she hadn't expected. Though, perhaps she should have. Perhaps she should have called him first instead of thinking this would be better dealt with face to face. If she'd called, she would have known he was going to be difficult and had a backup plan prepared.

Too late for that now. His tone had been hard, as had those aristocratic features, and there was no give in those deceptively hot golden eyes. He wasn't going to budge.

In which case you're going to need to be persuasive, aren't you?

Alice dragged her gaze away from him, turning plans over in her head. She wasn't leaving Spain without Diego, that was the bottom line. Her parents had passed away three years earlier—her mother to cancer and her father to a heart attack—which made Diego her only flesh and blood. And even apart from that, Emily had been very clear in her letter that she wanted Alice to look after her son. Especially now he'd been orphaned.

Sebastián was no relation and he was a hard, proud man. There was no softness in him, no warmth. He treated his horses better than he did people, and she didn't want Diego growing up with a father figure like that.

Children needed love and support and she had all of that to give. After all, she was never going to have a child herself, in which case Diego would be hers.

So getting Sebastián to change his mind might not be easy, but she wasn't going to leave without trying. Her nephew deserved that.

Alice didn't look back again. She turned from the corral and strode along the path through the gardens that led from the stables to the hacienda.

The house was massive, of whitewashed stone and a red-tiled roof, with many terraces and a central court-yard surrounded by colonnades shaded by lush grape vines and brilliant bougainvillea. Green lawns sur-rounded the house and gardens featuring banks of lav-ender, along with orange and olive trees and fountains. Out at the back of the house was the lavish pool area that Emily used to live in during the long hot sum-mers, or so she'd told Alice. Alice hadn't been here in summer. She and Edward had only visited in winter, when there was snow on the ground and the hacien-da's thick walls would hold in the warmth from the huge fireplace in the central living area.

She loved the estate, though she never let Emily or Edward know how much. She'd even tried to deny it to herself as well, because she didn't want to love anything of Sebastián's. Didn't want any ammunition that would fuel fantasies of how much better suited she was to living here than Emily.

Emily, who was afraid of the horses and complained of the isolation. Who wanted a bright, modern apartment in Paris, not some centuries-old, dark and dusty Spanish estate. Sebastián had duly bought her that Paris apartment and she'd spent a lot of time there, Alice knew. Probably to coincide with Edward's 'business trips'.

But she wasn't going to think of that, not about her sister and her husband. That way lay too much pain and she was barely getting by with grieving their loss, let alone their infidelity as well.

She walked through an archway that led into the central courtyard and then down a colonnaded path that ran down the side of the house before stepping through a door and into the cool of the wide hall.

Her suitcase was still standing beside the big wooden double front doors, as was her handbag. Well, it could stay there. She wasn't leaving.

She went down the hallway and into the huge living area. It was all low ceilings with exposed timber beams and stone flooring covered with thick rugs. Low couches upholstered in faded blue linen with thick white cushions were clustered around the giant fireplace, and dark wooden shelving lined the whitewashed walls.

It was wonderfully cool in here and she was tempted to sit down on one of the couches for a rest, because she was feeling overheated and dizzy, and still faintly nauseous. Then again, if she sat down, she wasn't going to get up again, and that wasn't going to help.

Besides, apart from anything, she wanted to see Diego.

Eventually, she tracked Lucia down in the kitchen. The housekeeper was putting something in the oven and, seeing Alice, she straightened and gave her a smile. 'Did you find Señor Sebastián?'

Alice smiled back. 'I did. But I have a problem, Lucia. I'm here to spend time with my nephew and I was silly. I didn't give either you or Sebastián any warning I was coming. So he's not very happy with me, I'm afraid.'

Lucia raised her hands. 'It's no problem. We have plenty of room. It is just Señor Sebastián and the little one now. And as for him not being happy with you...' She shrugged. 'He will get over it. You are not a stranger, after all.'

No, but she might as well be.

'Are you sure?' Alice didn't care about putting out Sebastián, but she didn't want to make things difficult for Lucia. 'There is a hotel in the village—'

'No, no,' Lucia interrupted emphatically. 'No, Señora Alice. You must stay here. I will not hear of you going to the village. No, absolutely not.'

It didn't matter how many times Alice had told Lucia to call her just Alice, the housekeeper insisted on calling her *señora*. It made her almost smile. Emily had loved Lucia, because Lucia liked taking care of people and Emily had loved being taken care of. Lucia was warm and motherly, and Alice had liked her too.

'Okay,' she said, feeling relief spread through her. 'I'd love that.'

'Good.' Lucia put down the tea towel she'd been holding. 'Now, I will get a room ready, but first you need food and something to drink. You have had a very long trip here, no?'

'Yes, it was very long.' Alice swallowed, feeling unaccountably nervous. 'Might I…see Diego?'

Lucia's smile became even warmer, the look in her dark eyes softening. 'He is having a nap now. And you, I think, need food, coffee and a rest.'

There was a fleeting moment's disappointment that she couldn't see him immediately, but she didn't want to wake him up, and it was true she'd really love a rest, so she let herself be taken charge of by Lucia instead.

Half an hour later, when Alice was feeling better after some food and a strong cup of coffee, Lucia showed her to one of the guest rooms. Without asking, she'd put Alice in a different room from the one she and Edward had normally used, which Alice was grateful for since she didn't need any more reminders.

It was a pretty room, too, with a terrace that overlooked the courtyard. The dark wooden French doors to the terrace stood open, allowing air to circulate, carrying with it the scent of lavender and the sound of the fountain.

A four-poster bed draped in white muslin was pushed up against one wall and covered in a thick white quilt, a pile of pillows resting against the carved headboard.

Alice sat down on it with some relief. She'd taken off her rumpled suit the moment Lucia had left, and had stepped into the en suite bathroom to have a cool shower. She felt better now, but there was still that deep-seated weariness that felt as if it had settled into her bones. Grief, naturally. It had been two months since Emily and Edward had died, but that exhaustion was still there, tugging at her.

She lay down on the soft quilt and put her head on the pillow, the cotton cool under her cheek. Yes, a rest was a good idea. She certainly was going to need all the energy she could get in order to face Sebastián again. Especially when he found out she hadn't left as he'd ordered her to.

It was only supposed to be a quick nap, but when Alice opened her eyes again, the room was full of the red-gold light of a long, European twilight. She must have slept half the day away and now it would probably be too late to see Diego. Still, she had to admit, she felt a lot better.

A good thing, considering a confrontation with Sebastián was on the cards.

Slipping off the bed, she went to her suitcase to find something to wear that wasn't a suit, only to see that on the low couch at the end of the bed had been laid a loose, cool-looking dress in faded red linen. It wasn't hers, which meant Lucia must have put it there for her.

Alice picked it up. The material was soft and silky, and with the loose style it looked as if it would fit. The faded red was a beautiful colour too. Where had Lucia found it? Was it Emily's? It probably wasn't, considering it wasn't Emily's colour, but then there were a lot of things she'd thought Emily wouldn't like and apparently had.

After a moment, she slipped the dress on and, indeed, it fitted beautifully, the red linen cool and soft against her skin. It was much less constricting than her suit, and she loved the feeling of the skirts swirling around her legs.

She didn't normally wear dresses. Emily was the pretty, feminine one. The one their father had doted on and their mother had called her 'little princess'. Alice had been the oldest and therefore the responsible one. Too independent and headstrong for their father and too tall and athletic to be anyone's little anything.

No one had called her anything but Alice, not even Edward.

Shaking out her still damp hair, Alice smoothed down the dress, then went to the door and opened it. She stepped into the hallway beyond and went down it to the big, dark wooden staircase that led downstairs.

Still thinking about what she was going to say to Sebastián, she didn't notice the man standing at the bottom of the stairs until it was too late.

He had his arms crossed over his muscular chest and he was watching her with hard golden eyes. 'What are you still doing here, Alice?'

* * *

At first all Sebastián could think about was how beautiful the red linen dress looked against her olive skin. How beautiful *she* looked, with her black hair loose and hanging in a glossy midnight tumble over her shoulders.

The dress was designed for comfort, not sex appeal and yet somehow, with her glorious height and Amazonian lines, Alice made it look effortlessly elegant.

He resented that. He resented the fact that she was still here at all.

Lucia had told him that Alice was staying in the way Lucia often did, as if this were her house and he had no say in the matter. And considering how long Lucia had been the housekeeper here, that was partially true. He'd never felt the need to argue with her before, but he did now and he resented that as well.

He didn't like having to pull the duke card with his staff and he wasn't about to start now, especially not when the problem was his sister-in-law.

Who apparently hadn't gone as he'd told her to.

She stopped halfway down the stairs and gave him an imperious look. 'What do you mean, what am I doing here? I presume Lucia told you?'

'She said you were staying. Which was not what I told you to do.'

'No, because I don't take kindly to being ordered around. Especially not after forty-eight hours of travel.'

Anger threaded through him. He didn't want her

here. She was too much of a reminder of all the things he'd sacrificed for the past five years, all the things he'd lost. His marriage, his wife, his future.

In Emily he'd thought he'd found the perfect bride. A woman who'd loved him, who'd needed him, who'd appealed to the protector in him and who'd wanted children eventually. And then he'd met Alice and realised he'd been mistaken in his choice. But divorcing Emily hadn't been possible, not for the honour of his family, and so he'd put all thoughts of Alice aside and concentrated on loving his wife instead.

At least, he'd tried. In fact, he'd thought he'd succeeded, until a business associate in Paris had told him he'd seen Emily out and about with her brother-in-law. Not that the signs hadn't been there before that, he'd just chosen to ignore them.

Regardless, Alice's presence brought all of that back and he wasn't having it.

'In that case,' he said curtly, 'you can stay the night. But in the morning, you need to leave.'

She was silent a moment, her guarded dark gaze expressionless. Then she said, 'No.' And folded her arms, mirroring his stance.

The thread of anger pulled tighter. 'What do you mean no?'

'Exactly what I said. I'm here for Diego, Sebastián, I told you that. And I'm not leaving without him.'

'And I told you that—'

'You will let me see him at least,' she interrupted, and there it was, deep in her eyes, that flicker of fire that had drawn him so strongly the moment they'd met. 'He's *my* nephew, Sebastián. He's the only family I've got.'

You can't deny her that.

He wanted to. He wanted to very badly. The longer she was here, the more her presence grated, and he didn't need that, not so soon after Emily's death. His life had already been upended once and he didn't need it happening again.

Then again, family was important, as Mateo, his father, had never ceased to tell him, though apparently that applied only to the Castellanos. And Sebastián was *not* a Castellano, which was another thing that Mateo never ceased to remind him of.

Still, it would be cruel to deny Alice the chance to meet her nephew, not to mention exceedingly petty. Emily had called him cruel once, and he supposed, to her, he had been. It was too late to make any recompense for that now, but he could allow Alice a day at least.

'Very well,' he said. 'You may have tomorrow. I expect you to leave the morning after.'

But instead of being satisfied with this as she should have been, Alice's black brows descended. 'Why?' she asked. 'What does it matter to you how long I stay?'

Good question. Pity he had no answer to give her, or at least not one that wouldn't betray exactly how much it mattered to him.

You're letting her get to you far too much.

Perhaps. Nevertheless, he'd decided.

'It doesn't matter,' he bit out. 'I've made my decision and that's final.'

She was silent again, watching him. Then, after a moment, she came down the rest of the stairs, the skirts of her dress swirling around her. She moved with such economical precision, as if once she had a direction to go in, nothing was going to get in her way.

He found it challenging and exciting in the way watching a spirited animal was challenging and exciting. Thinking about how to harness that animal's spirit, match it with his own, to help it grow and bloom into something magnificent.

You shouldn't be watching her.

No, he shouldn't. Yet he couldn't help himself.

She stopped in front of him, allowing some distance and yet still closer than he would have preferred. Not that he'd ever forget himself and grab her, but he didn't appreciate the temptation. The scent of sweet lavender surrounded him, probably from the soap made from the lavender flowers in the estate gardens that had been put in all the guest rooms. Emily hadn't liked it, preferring the more exotic and expensive scents she'd had made especially for her in Paris. He liked it though, and on Alice there was a sweetness beneath the lavender that made everything male in him sit up and take notice.

It had been a long time since he'd taken a woman to bed. He and Emily had grown apart in the months leading up to the accident and since then, grief and guilt had stolen away anything resembling desire.

But he could feel it now, rising in him as her scent wove around him and he watched the fire flicker in her dark eyes. He knew how badly he wanted to make that fire burn higher, hotter. It was a unique temptation, yet he couldn't give into it. He couldn't.

'You didn't say anything to me at Emily's funeral,' she said. 'Why was that?'

He knew he should step back, put some more distance between them, but he didn't. 'What did you want me to say?'

There was a flicker in her gaze, the glimpse of a temper she'd never displayed in his presence before, or at least not so openly. 'A hello might have been nice.'

But he hadn't said that. He hadn't said anything to her. Which had been rude, but he hadn't been able to bring himself to even approach her. She'd been wearing blue, Emily's favourite colour, in defiant opposition to the black all around her, and loss had been written all over her face. He should have said something, but he'd been so full of anger at Emily for betraying him, and at himself for his failure to make her happy, that he hadn't been able to trust himself to speak to anyone, let alone Alice.

Plus, he'd thought he'd never see her again after that and so what was the point?

'I'm sorry,' he said, knowing he sounded not sorry in the least, but unable to adjust his tone. 'I wasn't fit company that day.'

'Neither was I.'

He didn't like the challenging look in her eyes, not one bit. 'Is there a point to this?' he asked, because suddenly he was conscious that standing here too close to her wasn't a good idea. 'Dinner is ready in the courtyard and Lucia doesn't like people being late.'

Her dark eyes glittered. 'Fine. Let's have dinner. And you can tell me all about why you think Diego is better off here than he is with me.'

CHAPTER THREE

SEBASTIÁN DIDN'T LIKE that and it was obvious. Anger burned in the smoky golden depths of his eyes and his powerful body radiated tension. And heat. She could feel the warmth of him from where she stood; she hadn't realised quite how close to him she'd got, closer than she'd ever been before. She could smell him too, horse and dry earth, sunshine and hay, and under that something spicy and masculine that made her whole body tighten with want.

He was so much taller than she was, his shoulders wide and his chest broad. He made her feel petite and fragile, and while a part of her hated that, another part, the part that had always wanted to be the same delicate, pretty little princess that her sister was, loved it.

Heat climbed in her face, her heartbeat accelerating. A mistake to get so close. She needed to put some distance between them before she gave herself away.

Except he was the one who turned abruptly and strode off in the direction of the courtyard without a backward glance.

Alice swallowed and tried to control her thumping

heart. She couldn't get that close to him again. She was too susceptible and if she wasn't careful, she'd end up taking her eye off her goal. It was Diego who was important, and she couldn't forget that.

Emily had wanted him brought home to New Zealand. Emily had wanted him to grow up loved.

In her letter she had written:

I'm so sorry to put you in this position and I know it's asking a lot. You may not ever forgive me for what I did and I'm not asking you to. I wouldn't if I were you. But this isn't about me. This is about Diego. And I'm afraid of what Sebastián will do if he finds out Diego isn't his.

He won't hurt him—he's not violent. But he's cold and proud and blood means everything to him. I want Diego to grow up loved...

Well, Sebastián was certainly proud, but it hadn't been ice in his eyes when he'd spoken of Diego. It had been fire. She could almost imagine him as an ancient warrior with a sword in hand, defending his family, his home, from any invaders who dared cross his threshold.

Emily hadn't said much about their marriage, but Alice had often had the feeling her sister wasn't happy. It was obvious now, of course, since she'd been having an affair with Edward, but Alice wondered what it was that had made Emily so unhappy. Sebastián was a duke, with an ancient lineage and centuries of wealth behind him, and he was gorgeous. Emily liked status and money and a pretty face. She liked having some-one being possessive and protective, but…

Why had she thought Sebastián cold? Why did she fear him bringing Diego up? Was it something to do with their own father? Emily had been his fa-vourite—he hadn't known what to do with tall, stub-born Alice—and he'd doted on her. Maybe that was it. Maybe all she'd wanted was for her son to have a father who doted on him the way their father had doted on her.

Well, whatever her reasons were, Alice was going to have her work cut out for her if she was going to change Sebastián's mind, that was for sure.

She took a breath and followed him into the court-yard.

Outside, under the shade of a trellis trailing bou-gainvillea, was a wooden table neatly set with a white tablecloth, plates and cutlery, and stemless wine glasses. The heat of the day had faded, leaving be-hind a warm, pleasant twilight, the air scented with lavender.

Lucia was setting out plates of food that smelled absolutely delicious. Sebastián stood near her, saying something in Spanish that it was clear she did not like one bit. She frowned at him, replying in stern tones as if she was telling him off about something.

Alice tensed. He was already burning with anger, which meant surely Lucia was taking her life into her own hands speaking to him like that.

He glared at her and said something else in a hard,

curt voice. Lucia merely shrugged, unbothered. Then, noticing Alice standing there, she said in English, 'It is rude to talk in Spanish when Señora Alice cannot understand us, Señor Sebastián.' She looked at him sternly, and added, 'I have cooked a meal for you both, and you will sit down and eat it. Together.'

Alice blinked. She'd never seen Sebastián be told what to do and for a moment she wondered what on earth Lucia was thinking. His carved features were set in uncompromising lines, his hard mouth unyielding. His golden eyes burned with sullen fury.

Alice waited for him to launch into a verbal attack, maybe even fire his housekeeper on the spot, yet instead he muttered something short and sharp in Spanish, went over to the table, pulled out a chair and sat down.

'Manners, Señor Sebastián,' Lucia murmured.

He muttered another curse, got to his feet, moved over to the chair opposite his, pulled it out and looked fiercely at Alice. 'Please,' he said, his voice like iron. 'Won't you join me for dinner?'

A small shock arrowed down her spine. It seemed that this hard, proud man had not only been roundly told off by his housekeeper, he was also doing exactly what she said, albeit with all the grace of a sullen teenager.

Alice almost wanted to smile.

Lucia, who didn't seem in imminent danger of being fired and obviously wasn't afraid of Sebastián in any way, gave an approving nod, gathered up her trays, and disappeared back into the hacienda.

Sebastián remained standing rigidly behind the chair he'd pulled out. He looked as if he wanted to bite someone's head off.

Alice took another silent breath then moved over to the table. 'I had no idea Lucia was so fierce,' she said as she sat down, trying to keep her voice light.

'She doesn't like it when her meals are under-appreciated.' Sebastián's tone was hard as rock, but Alice could feel the masculine heat of him at her back, smell his delicious scent. It made her mouth go dry.

'Don't feel you have to sit and eat with me,' she said as he pushed her chair in for her. 'I'm sure you have plenty of other things to do.'

'Lucia wants us to eat together.' He came around the table and sat down opposite her. 'The hospitality of the ancient dukes is important to her and we have certain standards to uphold.' He glowered across the table at her. 'Especially to "family".'

This was clearly going to be so much harder than she'd thought. So much. His anger and resentment seemed to reach across the table and wrap around her throat, choking her.

But she wasn't Emily. She wasn't going to crumble and weep in the face of male temper. She often had to deal with that at her company and she'd never let it intimidate her before. She wasn't going to let it now.

Calmly, she picked up one of the snowy white napkins and shook it out over her lap. 'And what? You do everything she says?'

His gaze sharpened, cutting like a knife. 'She has been here for decades and is part of the family. I value her so, yes, on occasion I do what she says.' He said it as if this were self-evident and she was stupid for not understanding. Which of course made her bristle with annoyance.

Except she wasn't going to rise to his bad temper. Men could be so overly emotional sometimes and maybe this was doubly true of Spanish men.

You like his passion. You've always liked it.

In those early days after Emily had first married him, Alice had received lots of glowing emails from her sister about how attentive and protective Sebastián was. Emily had also overshared about his demands in bed and how thrilling that was. Alice had determinedly shoved away her envy, choked her jealousy, and shut down any fevered fantasies about what it would be like to be in Sebastian's arms herself.

She had been married to Edward, who had been loving and attentive with her even after they'd lost the baby. In fact, he'd been very careful and gentle and while she'd been recovering that had been exactly what she'd wanted. But years past the loss—at least physically—what she'd wanted was passion. Desperation. Possession. She'd wanted Edward to be hungry for her, desire her feverishly. She'd wanted to feel as though she was still attractive to him instead of an empty vessel, her fertility gone and her dreams of a family along with them.

But he hadn't been hungry for her, as it had turned out. He'd been hungry for her sister and who could blame him? Emily, petite and feminine and fertile, everything that Alice wasn't.

Edward had been a childhood friend of both her and Emily, and she'd had a crush on him for years. Except he'd only had eyes for Emily. And then Emily had left to go to university in Australia, leaving Edward behind with Alice, and the two of them had grown closer. Alice had been thrilled when he'd told her that he'd fallen in love with her and then asked her to marry him.

Her instead of Emily. Not that Emily had been jealous. No, she'd been Alice's bridesmaid at the wedding and had given the loveliest speech. Except…he'd obviously had second thoughts, hadn't he?

But Alice couldn't bear thinking about that particular past. It was futile. Edward was gone, and so was Emily, and all she had left was Diego.

'Well,' she said in a cool voice. 'Lucia is not here now, so please don't stay on my account.'

Sebastian's gaze didn't even flicker. 'You wanted to talk about Diego.' He made a gesture with one long-fingered hand. 'So. Talk.'

He didn't want to be here. He didn't want to sit opposite her and talk about how Diego would be better off going back to New Zealand with her. He didn't want to talk to her at all.

But Lucia had insisted and he wasn't so petty as to put aside the wishes of a loyal and valued employee. It was only one dinner and he could handle that and, besides, it was probably useful to get the subject of Diego over and done with now.

Then tomorrow, with any luck, Alice could leave.

'Fine,' she said with that irritating cool that got under his skin so badly. 'Why do you want Diego to stay with you?'

He'd already told her his reasons, but if she wanted him to repeat them then fine, he would.

He picked up the bottle of wine on the table and leaned forward, pouring some into her glass before doing the same for himself. 'He is my son. What other reason is there?'

'But…he's not actually your son, is he? He's Emily and Edward's.'

There was no denying that, though Sebastián preferred to keep that secret to himself. Easy enough when everyone thought Diego was his anyway. There had been some rumours, some mutterings about an affair in the elite circles he moved in after Emily had died, but he'd shut them down hard before they could gain traction.

No one was going to take Diego from him and that was final. Of course, Sebastián would tell him when he got older who his parents were and that he could find out more about them. After all, Sebastián wasn't like Mateo, his father, who'd hidden the identity of Sebastián's biological father from him, refusing to tell him anything about him. Sebastián would never be so cruel. But there was no other reason to give him up. Edward had no family and Emily's parents were dead. The only problem was Alice, who seemed to think she had a better claim on him.

'They aren't here,' he said with finality. 'But I am.'

'In case it's escaped your notice, so am I.' Her voice was as level and cool as her gaze. 'Emily's letter said that—'

'I don't care about Emily's letter,' he interrupted, his temper starting to slip the leash. 'Diego was born here, in the hacienda. I was there. I held him. He carries my name. He is my son, my heir, and there is nothing more to be said.'

This time her gaze flickered and she looked down at her wine, picking it up and taking a sip. Faint colour stained her cheekbones. In the rose and gold of twilight, her skin looked luminous, lit from within, her hair glossy and soft. She was so different from Emily's honey-haired fragility and he didn't know why she appealed to him on such a gut-deep level. It didn't make any sense.

Emily had. He'd seen her on the terrace of a hotel in Madrid, enjoying a glass of wine and laughing with a friend. She'd been so pretty and joyful, and at that point in his life, after his father had so recently died, he'd needed joy. He'd been feeling the weight of the dukedom on his shoulders and, initially, she'd been only an escape for him, a distraction.

But after he'd spent more time with her and she'd told him of her dreams of having a family and a place to put down roots, he'd decided that she would be his new duchess. She hadn't made him feel as if he was missing something vital from his make-up, the way his father always had. She'd made him feel as if he was everything his father had always wanted, the scion of an ancient house. Proud. Strong. Honourable. As if the purest noble blood ran in his veins instead of that of the stable hand his mother had had an affair with.

The stable hand he'd had much more in common with than the man who'd brought him up.

'Emily was my sister,' Alice said. 'And I'm sorry, but there is plenty more to be said.' She reached down, brought out a piece of folded paper from the pocket of her dress, and held it out to him. 'Read this.'

He didn't look at the letter, only stared at her. 'Emily's letter, I presume?'

She nodded.

'And what does it say?' He tried to keep his tone even. 'That she was afraid to leave her son with me?'

'Read it, Sebastián.'

'No.' What was the point, when he knew what was in it already? 'I don't need to. She told you I would make a terrible father, didn't she?'

Alice let out a breath and put the letter down in the middle of the table. Then she fussed with her napkin. 'She said she wanted him to grow up...loved.'

Something twisted painfully inside him, but he made sure nothing showed on his face. He deserved that. They'd never spoken of the hole in the centre of their marriage. Emily had avoided any conversation about it because she hated confrontations, and since confrontations inevitably resulted in Emily weeping, so had he.

But he knew Emily had wanted more from him. She'd wanted love. He'd given her what he could, yet it hadn't been enough. She'd known he was holding something back, and he had been.

His heart. Because the problem was that love, in his experience, was mean and petty and cruel, and he'd wanted nothing to do with it.

Then he'd met Alice and what he'd felt for her, he'd never been able to pin down. He'd never wanted to. It had felt too obsessive, too painful, and so he'd put it aside. Now all that was left was physical desire— somehow that hadn't faded the way the other emotions had. That and the only love he'd ever permitted himself, for a little baby who wasn't even his.

She should have known you'd love him. She should.

No, she shouldn't. Why would she? She'd only wanted what any wife wanted from their husband, and he'd failed her. This letter and the pain that came with it were his punishment.

You should give Diego to Alice and be done with it.

Except every cell in his body rebelled against that thought. He wasn't giving up his son. Diego *was* his.

He'd claimed him and a Castellano duke never gave up what was his.

Alice had gone still, watching him from across the table. What she saw he didn't know, until she said, 'I'm sorry. She only wanted what was best for her son and she thought him being in New Zealand was best for him.'

So, he hadn't hidden his grief and pain as well as he thought. He didn't like that she could read him and far more easily than Emily ever had.

She thinks Emily was right, that it's better for Diego to go back to New Zealand with her.

His heart twisted again as if in protest, though, really, why should it matter what Alice thought of him? He wanted her, it was true, and he always had, but all the other powerful feelings she'd managed to evoke had gone. He'd starved them completely. So it shouldn't matter. It shouldn't matter at all.

The urge to explain himself was still strong, but he shoved it aside, reaching for the cold, hard manner that had served him so well in the past. The manner his father had insisted on since that was the manner of a duke, not a common stable hand.

Sebastián leaned back in his chair and met her level gaze. There was a softness in her dark eyes that hadn't been there before. *Dios.* Did she feel sorry for him? Well, there was no need. He wasn't giving up his son—yes, *his* son. Not for anything.

'Why do you want him?' he asked instead. 'What is he to you?'

Her eyes widened slightly in surprise. 'I would have thought that was obvious. He's my nephew, Sebastián.'

Her calm was infuriating. 'So?'

'So?' Finally, as he'd seen out by the corral and on the stairs, fire flickered in her gaze. 'Like I told you, he's all I have left of Emily.'

'Blood is the only reason, then?' he demanded. 'Because your sister was his mother and your husband his father? What do you know of *him* though? Do you know that he takes a little time to settle and that he loves a Spanish lullaby? That he also likes the sound of horses' hooves during the day and will only nap if he can hear them? Do you know that his first smile was three weeks ago and for me? And that when he cries, sometimes only I can settle him?'

Something crossed her face then and it wasn't that cool, calm expression she'd been giving him. It was sharper, flickers of pain and grief.

Do you really think she's untouched by this? That she doesn't care? You know she does.

Before he'd met Alice and shut down all conversation about her with Emily, his wife had told him about her tall, practical older sister. It hadn't been entirely complimentary and he'd envisaged a stodgy, humourless, dull sort of woman. Except that hadn't been the case. The two sisters had had a fractious relationship, it seemed, and yet it was clear that the pair of them had loved each other dearly despite it.

Of course this would affect Alice and he couldn't ignore that, no matter how much he wanted to.

She is passionate too, remember?

A memory surfaced, making his heartbeat suddenly fast. Of the last Christmas that Alice and Edward had come to the hacienda. It had been Christmas Eve and they'd all been in the living room sipping eggnog. It had been late, but he'd gone out to deal with an urgent matter in the stables, and when he'd come back, everyone else had gone to bed leaving only Alice standing by the fire, staring down at it.

What she'd been wearing, he couldn't remember, but he remembered every contour of her face and how the fire lit her as though she'd been painted with gold. The curve of her cheek. The lush dark fan of her lashes. The fullness of her bottom lip. And the sadness in her expression that had reached inside him and twisted hard.

He'd wanted to know what had made her so sad. He'd wanted to know everything, and then he'd wanted to fix it. And only after that had he wanted to take her in his arms and make her forget whatever it was that had caused her so much grief, wake the passion that he knew was inside her.

Except she hadn't been his and he hadn't been hers and he hadn't been able to do any of those things.

She'd looked up in that moment and their eyes had met. And whatever that thing was between them, the instant connection, the passionate energy, had suddenly sung in the room.

For one long minute they'd stared at one another and he'd seen the look in her eyes catch fire, and he'd known that if they'd both been free to choose, nothing could have kept them apart.

But they hadn't been free, and he was as wedded to his honour as much as he had been to Emily, and so choice hadn't been an option for him.

So he'd turned and walked away.

He wanted to walk away now but... He couldn't. Regardless of how sorry he felt for her, he wasn't going to let Diego go and the sooner she understood that, the better.

'I do care about him,' she said quietly. 'That's why I wanted to take him home. The country his parents came from, to the family that—'

'He was born Spanish. He *is* Spanish. And *I* am his family.'

Her jaw firmed and a spark leapt in her gaze, hot and burning. And he felt the same fire in him respond.

He should look away, he really should.

'I'm not leaving, Sebastián,' she said fiercely. 'I want to see my nephew and I will see him. You're not going to stop me.'

The sun was behind him, sending long fingers of light across her face, bathing it in glory. She wasn't typically beautiful, not as Emily had been. It was her spirit that was beautiful, that caught him by the throat and refused to let go. That made him want to sweep away all the dishes on Lucia's perfectly set table and grab her, haul her over it and into his arms. Put his mouth on hers and finally ease the hunger of years.

But he didn't. He couldn't. Following his own

wants and needs had always been a mistake, and he wasn't going to start now. Besides, he had the honour of the Castellanos to uphold, and dukes did not do such things.

What does it matter if she sees him? Dukes aren't petty either, they are capable of justice and magnanimity.

He could do that. He could allow her to stay, and once she'd seen Diego and spent time with him she'd leave. In the meantime, he'd simply keep his distance from her. And if she insisted once again on taking Diego, he'd get his lawyers to deal with her. That way they could avoid any dangerous situations like this one, where anger only fuelled the fire that burned between them.

'Fine,' he said, his voice little more than a growl. 'You have three days. No longer.'

Then he did the only other thing he could.

He shoved back his chair and walked away.

CHAPTER FOUR

THE NEXT MORNING Alice sat in the dim, cool living room of the hacienda, a ball of nervous tension sitting in her gut. Her palms were sweaty and her heartbeat loud.

It was silly to feel so nervous about meeting a four-month-old baby, but she couldn't help it. She'd read all the books she'd been able to lay her hands on about babies when she was pregnant the first time, so it wasn't that she didn't know what to expect. It was only she had no actual practical experience with children, and what if she was terrible at it? What if she dropped him? What if he cried and refused to be comforted?

Emily hadn't called her at all after his birth, but she had emailed, and the only thing Alice had known about him from those emails was that he was a good baby who settled well and hardly ever cried.

'Do you know that he takes a little time to settle and that he loves a Spanish lullaby? That he also likes the sound of horses' hooves during the day and will only nap if he can hear them? Do you know that his first

smile was three weeks ago and for me? And that when he cries, sometimes only I can settle him?'

Sebastián's voice from the night before at their aborted dinner drifted through her head, deep and fierce. His expression had been hard yet the smoky gold of his eyes had shone like pirates' treasure at the bottom of a dark sea.

Her mouth had gone dry then, even as her own anger at him and his intransigence had leapt. He just... burned. He was that warrior with a sword in his hand and a baby in his arms, determined to protect. Determined to keep.

All she'd been able to think about was how hungry she was for a piece of that determination, that possessiveness. Because Edward hadn't had either, or, if he had, he'd never displayed it towards her.

He'd told her after she'd lost the baby, after she'd lost any hope of having a family of her own, that it would all be fine. They could adopt or even have a surrogate, anything she wanted. Yet every time she'd try bringing the subject of a child up again, he'd wave her gently away or agree vaguely, and then never follow up on it. He hadn't touched her the way he once had, either. Sex had become perfunctory, as if he'd been doing it because he'd had to, not because he'd wanted to. And then, in the last year, they hadn't had sex at all.

She'd always had issues around her femininity, largely driven by her parents' constant comparison— even if unconscious—to Emily, and in the last year of their marriage, Edward had made her feel as if she'd actively repulsed him. She'd tried to talk with him about it but he hadn't been interested, and it hadn't been until the car accident and Emily's letter that she'd found out why.

Edward had had a child with another woman. Her sister.

But she couldn't think about that now. It hurt too much and, anyway, her feelings about the whole thing weren't important. Only Diego was.

She took a breath as Sofia, his nanny, came into the room, a small wrapped bundle in her arms.

Alice got to her feet, resisting the urge to wipe her hands down the front of her denim shorts.

Sofia said something soft in Spanish that Alice didn't understand—Lucia had told her that Sofia didn't speak English—and then put the little bundle into Alice's arms with an encouraging smile.

He was heavier than Alice had expected and warmer too.

She looked down into his face and met Emily's wide blue eyes staring back at her.

Her throat closed, her vision full of unexpected tears, but she forced them back. Perhaps she should have expected the likeness but she hadn't, and the complex wave of grief and joy that swamped her took her by surprise.

And there was joy. This little person was Emily's and, by extension of blood, hers, too, and the emotion that filled her, a powerful love, made Sebastián's ferocity about him suddenly understandable.

He felt this way about Diego too and so... How could she take Diego away from him? Yet also, how could she leave Diego herself?

The baby had settled against her and all her nerves had gone. Not that she knew any more about babies than she had a moment before, she was just even more certain that she couldn't leave him. She wouldn't. Three days, Sebastián had told her, but it wasn't enough. Which meant she was left with two choices: either she initiated proceedings with her lawyers to get Diego home or...she stayed here in Spain until she and Sebastián could work out some kind of custody arrangement.

Slowly, still cradling the little boy in her arms, Alice turned towards the windows and walked towards them. Her nephew's eyes were very wide, looking up into hers, and her heart contracted. She had a life back in New Zealand, but it wasn't much of one, only her, rattling around in the house in Auckland she and Edward had bought. There was her investment company and that was far more successful, but it could keep. She could also work remotely.

What else could she do?

Diego was Emily's and he had her eyes, and, even though Emily had wanted him to be brought back to New Zealand, Sebastián had a point. This couldn't be about what Emily wanted, but what was right for Diego. Not when Emily was dead. Still, her sister was right about one thing: this little boy needed to be loved and while Sebastián was certainly possessive, could he give Diego the love that he needed? Perhaps he could. Perhaps Emily's worries about him were unfounded and unfair. Regardless, Alice was also certain that her nephew needed a mother.

She looked down into his little face, seeing traces of Emily in his nose and in the delicacy of his mouth.

His own mother was gone now, but Alice was here. She could be that for him. She would *always* be that for him. Fathers could be difficult and sometimes harsh, and that needed to be balanced out with someone who could accept him no matter what.

Not that her own mother had been any more accepting of her, but at least she'd shown Alice what *not* to do. All a child really needed was to know that they were loved, and she had plenty of love to give. She would give it to Diego.

She spent a half-hour with the baby, just holding him and getting familiar with him, and when it was time for him to go down for a nap, she let the nanny take him.

As much as she wished she could, there was no point putting off the conversation she needed to have with Sebastián. He had to know immediately that she was intending to stay longer than three days. He wouldn't like it—he'd already made his feelings about her presence here known—but that was too bad. He'd have to deal with it.

After a cursory look around the hacienda failed to locate him, she went down to the stables. But he wasn't there either. Then, as she was coming back to the house, she heard the distinctive sound of helicopter rotors. There was a helipad not far from the house and, since any helicopter around was likely to be for him, she headed in that direction.

Sure enough, she arrived at the helipad in time to see him striding along the path from the house in the direction of the chopper. And despite herself, her breath caught.

He was in a suit today, perfectly tailored to highlight his height and muscled physique. It was of dark blue wool and he wore a black business shirt with it and a blue silk tie. Darkly handsome, phenomenally arrogant and every inch the Spanish duke, his golden eyes smouldering like distant fires, he almost stopped her in her tracks.

Stupid of her. She couldn't let him get to her, especially with the well-being of her nephew at stake.

With an effort, Alice threw off the paralysing effect of his charisma, and called, 'Sebastián! I need a moment.'

He came to a stop and glanced at her as she approached, his gaze raking her from head to toe. She could feel herself start to blush, which was infuriating. Compared to him, all dark beauty and athletic grace, she felt dowdy and frumpy, and she resented it. She wished she'd worn the red dress today, but Lucia had taken it to be washed, and so she'd flung on a baggy pair of denim shorts and a loose black T-shirt. Emily had always dressed herself to the nines because she'd said that Sebastián 'liked it'. What he must think of her current outfit she had no idea and didn't particularly want to know either.

'What do you want?' he asked coldly. 'Be quick, please.'

Alice tried to calm her frantically beating heart. 'We need to talk more about Diego.'

His expression darkened. 'Do we? I thought we said everything we needed to last night.'

'You might have,' Alice snapped, needled by his tone. 'But I didn't.'

Sebastián glanced towards the helicopter then back at her. 'Well, it will have to wait. I'm leaving on a business trip and I need to go now. You can call me when you get back to New Zealand.'

'No, I won't be calling you, because I'm not actually leaving,' Alice informed him flatly. 'Three days isn't enough time, Sebastián. Diego needs a mother in his life and, since Emily is gone, I've decided to be that mother.'

His hard handsome features remained still, carved out of stone. Only his golden eyes burned. 'That option is not available—'

'I'm staying,' she interrupted. 'I'm not leaving him.'

A muscle leapt in his jaw. 'If I find you still here when I return, I will have you arrested for trespassing.'

Alice's temper began to slip through her fingers. 'Do it, then,' she shot back. 'I'll pitch a tent here on the lawn.'

The pilot of the helicopter appeared suddenly at Sebastián's elbow and said something to him in a low voice. Sebastián nodded curtly then glanced back at Alice. 'I haven't got time to talk about this now. We will discuss it—'

He broke off as Alice turned from him and started furiously towards the helicopter. Because one thing was clear; he was only going to keep fobbing her off or walking away, and she was tired of it. She hadn't come all the way here just to be told what to do by Sebastián Castellano. She had come for her nephew, and they were *going* to talk about him, business trip or not.

A discussion needed to be had, an agreement come to, and they would come to it even if she had to go with him on his stupid business trip herself.

The pilot came rushing after her, but if he'd been intending to stop her he was too late, because by the time he arrived, Alice had already climbed into the helicopter and had belted herself in.

Sebastián halted by the open helicopter door and stared at her. 'What the hell are you doing, Alice?' he demanded.

'Coming with you,' she said, daring him to protest. 'If you won't stay and have this conversation with me here, I'll come with you and have it there.'

'You will do no such thing,' he growled, anger disturbing the ice in his voice, his accent more pronounced. 'Get out of the helicopter right now.'

'No.' Alice lifted her chin. 'If you want me out, you'll have to pull me out yourself.'

Fury burned in his eyes, his body full of a coiled tension that was almost palpable, and for a minute she wondered if she'd made a mistake and if he would actually pull her out himself. Then the pilot said something to him, and he cursed again, low and vicious. Then he said, 'Fine. *Vámonos.*' And got into the helicopter and pulled the door shut.

It was only then that Alice realised that she *had* in fact made a mistake. A terrible one. Because as soon as the door closed, she was locked into the helicopter with him and it was a small space. He was right next to her, the warmth of one powerful thigh almost touching hers, and she was surrounded by his delicious scent; masculine spice, sunlight, and hay.

Her mouth dried and her stomach dipped as he held out a headset without glancing at her.

Okay, so this was actually going to happen, was it? He'd called her bluff and now they were actually going to…

'I… I need to get a bag,' she said, trying not to sound so hesitating.

Only then did he glance at her. 'Too late. We need to leave now because we're going to lose our weather window.'

'But I—'

'You wanted to come, so you're coming.' One black brow rose. 'Or have you changed your mind?'

He wanted her to change her mind; she could see it in his eyes. He wanted her to give in and get out of the helicopter. And maybe she should. Maybe she could wait to have this conversation when he returned.

But he was right. It was too late. She couldn't back down now and she wasn't going to.

Alice held his gaze and grabbed the headset from him. 'No, of course not. So where are we going?'

'Madrid.'

Shutting himself into a confined space for the couple of hours it would take them to fly to Madrid, and then to spend the duration of his business trip with his sister-in-law, was likely to be a mistake, and Sebastián was well aware.

But she'd left him with no choice.

He was hardly going to manhandle her out of the helicopter and even though he would dearly have loved to leave her sitting in it for the next couple of hours, the pilot had been very clear about the window they had for departure. There was a storm coming in over the mountains and they had to go now.

She hadn't been expecting him to call her bluff, that was certain, not given the way her dark eyes had widened as he'd climbed in beside her and shut the door. But she'd covered her shock very well, her chin determined, her expression set, her lush mouth in a hard line.

Maybe it was for the best in the end. They couldn't keep having the same conversation and he was tired of her pushing him on it. He could involve the police to get her removed from the house if she continued to be difficult, but he didn't want to do that. Lucia would be appalled, and Alice was his sister-in-law after all.

She wasn't going to be put off, which meant he was going to have to sit down with her and come to some arrangement about Diego. Some kind of civilised arrangement.

The only problem was that he didn't feel particularly civilised, not with her sitting next to him, wearing only a pair of denim shorts and a loose black T-shirt that was so thin he could see the lace of her bra. Her legs were long and tanned and smooth, and they were sitting close enough that her bare skin nearly brushed the wool of his suit trousers.

He could barely think, and he was furious with himself.

He'd thought he'd made himself clear when he'd walked away from the dinner table the night before. Yet he should have known that she wouldn't meekly do what he said, that she wouldn't stay the requisite three days and then leave. And he thought he'd been smart in taking this business trip over the time she would be staying so he didn't have to have more contact with her. Except it hadn't turned out that way and he still couldn't understand how it had got away from him.

He only knew that he hadn't taken into account her sheer stubbornness and now he was dealing with the consequences. Which were Alice, sitting next to him in a helicopter for two hours, one bare thigh pressed against his, and him as breathless as a teenage boy with his first crush.

The pilot had got in and was spinning up the rotors, and the moment where he could have got rid of her was gone. So, he put on his headset and tried to ignore her as they lifted off smoothly, climbing into the sky, heading for the mountains.

'So,' Alice's voice came crisply through the headset, 'Diego needs a mother, Sebastián. You do know that, don't you?'

He'd been going to work on the trip to Madrid, but with her sitting next to him there was no hope of that. 'We can talk about this when we get to Madrid,' he said curtly.

'If this is a two-hour trip then we might as well discuss it now.'

Sebastián gritted his teeth. 'Diego has Sofia. Until I—'

'Sofia, I'm sure, is a faultless nanny, but she's not his mother.'

'No, his mother is dead,' he bit out. 'And if you'd let me finish, I would have told you that he will have a mother eventually. When I remarry.'

There was a shocked silence that satisfied him far too much and yet made him feel guilty at the same time. It was too soon after Emily's death to even contemplate, but he had to. With his wife gone, he needed to remarry, because Alice was right, Diego did need a mother. Sebastián's own mother had died when he was born so he'd grown up without one, his cold, distant father his only parent. He didn't want that for his son. Not that he had any intention of being like Mateo, but a child should have at least some maternal influence in their life.

Also, he wanted more children. Diego was his heir, despite not being of Sebastián's own blood, which was fine. Sebastián was not Mateo's biological son after all. But he had been an only child and it had been lonely. Diego should have siblings.

'Remarry?' Alice echoed. 'But Emily is only two—'

'Months gone?' he interrupted. 'Yes, I'm well aware. Still, I need more than one heir and you're right, Diego does need a mother. In which case I'm going to need another wife.'

'Emily said you were cold. I had no idea just how much.'

He glanced at her and her dark eyes met his, the expression in them furious. He couldn't blame her. He *was* cold. His heart had always led him astray and so he had to be careful. Mateo had been very clear what was expected of a duke and that was not to allow his emotions to get the better of him.

Yet it was difficult to hear what his own wife had accused him of on more than one occasion coming out of Alice's mouth.

'You're so cold,' Emily had said a couple of times. *'Don't you care about anything?'*

But he had cared, that was the problem. He'd cared too much and, unfortunately for Emily, it wasn't her that he'd cared about, not as intensely as he'd cared about Alice.

'I prefer practical,' he said, wrestling with his own

temper. 'I have responsibilities now and I need to keep Diego's future in mind.'

Anger flickered in her eyes. 'Oh? Until you have a child of your own blood, you mean?'

Sebastián stared at her a long moment. Did she really think that was what his issue was? Apparently so. Well, he needed to disabuse her of that notion. 'No,' he said. 'Diego is my heir and will remain so, no matter how many other children I have. But I don't want him to grow up an only child. He should have siblings.'

Alice didn't reply immediately, but her gaze was searching. Did she not believe him? Did she really think he would lie about this?

Are you surprised? She doesn't know you, remember? You can't blame her for having a low opinion of you when you cultivated that yourself.

A shiver of electricity moved through him, though why he had no idea. Because it was true. He'd deliberately made himself unpleasant when it came to her. He was never openly rude but was always subtly cold. Distant. Making sure she never got too close.

No wonder she thinks Diego would be better off with her. And no wonder she believed what Emily told her about you.

'Siblings?' she asked. 'That's really the only reason? Come on, Sebastián. You can't tell me you wouldn't disinherit him in a second if you had a child of your own blood.'

A flicker of pain went through him, though he could think of no earthly reason why, when what she thought of him didn't matter in the slightest. He'd never given her reason to think differently and what was the point now?

However, she still seemed to believe that Diego was unimportant to him and he really couldn't let that stand.

'I see you believe every word Emily told you about me,' he said. 'And that she didn't tell you anything about my history.'

A small crease appeared between Alice's eyebrows. 'What history?'

He didn't tell people about his true origins. His father had guarded the secret jealously and, after Mateo had passed away, so had he. Even now, even after the rumours about him had largely disappeared, only Emily had known the truth. He'd sworn her to secrecy and it was clear she hadn't told her sister a thing. Perhaps he shouldn't let Alice know now. Then again, if he did, she'd understand how he felt about Diego. Perhaps she'd then go home and leave him in peace.

'I am not actually my father's son by blood,' he said. 'A childhood illness left him sterile, but he needed an heir and so when he found out about my mother's affair with a stable hand, and that she was pregnant because of it, he raised the child as his own.'

Alice's eyes widened. 'You?'

'Yes. No one ever knew I wasn't Mateo's son. He made sure of it.'

She looked shocked. 'Did Emily know?'

'Of course.'

'And Diego…'

'Will be my heir. I'll bring him up as my own son and, no, it won't make any difference if I have children of my own blood.'

'So you'll treat him the way your father treated you?'

'No,' he snapped before he could stop himself. 'I would never do that.'

Something shifted in her gaze, though he wasn't sure what it was. Interest perhaps, or curiosity. 'Why? How did your father treat you?'

But he wasn't going to have that conversation, not with her. 'It doesn't matter. All that matters is that Diego will not be disadvantaged because he is not biologically related to me. He will be my son in every other way.'

She didn't say anything immediately, the expression in her gaze unreadable.

'You have my word,' he added, because if she was searching for the truth then he'd give it to her. She needed to know that, while he might have failed Emily, he wouldn't fail Diego.

It had never been a good idea to look into her dark eyes for too long and he knew he shouldn't look now. He didn't want her to see the need burning in him for her. He had to keep it locked away. It would be a disaster if she knew, because then…

Then you might throw caution to the winds? Say 'to hell with it' and take her? Ignore your control and give your heart what it wants instead?

He could. His wife was gone and there was nothing stopping him now. Nothing but the years of denial and guilt and relentless self-control. Nothing but his father's constant, painful example of how love and desire could eat you alive from the inside out and turn you into someone vindictive and cruel and petty.

He wouldn't follow that example. He'd spent years trying to do the right thing, the honourable thing, because he was a Castellano duke and Castellano dukes were always honourable. He couldn't allow those years to be wasted on something so ephemeral and meaningless as sex. And that was all it would be. Just sex and nothing more. *Dios*, if he wanted a woman, he'd find someone else. Someone far less complicated than Alice.

So he kept tight control of himself and it was she who looked away, glancing out of the window, colour staining the olive skin of her cheekbones.

Curious that he'd made her blush, not that he should have noticed.

'You're not who I thought you were,' she said after a moment.

He studied the curve of her cheek and the fan of delicate dark lashes almost resting on it. They were very long, those lashes, and silky looking. 'And who did you think I was?'

'Someone who'd let Diego go easily. I thought that you wouldn't want him because he's not yours.'

He shouldn't keep looking at her, and yet he couldn't stop. The sun through the window was glossing her dark hair. She had it in a low ponytail at the back of her neck and he couldn't help noting that the T-shirt she wore was faded. Old clothes. She really hadn't expected to be going anywhere today, had she?

'Well,' he said. 'You thought wrong.'

Her eyes had widened, and they were even darker, her pupils dilating. Abruptly the tension between them pulled tight, the air in the helicopter filling with a crackling heat.

The colour in her cheeks deepened and a startled expression flickered through her velvet dark eyes, as if she'd read every thought in his head, and that was bad, very bad. He'd wondered, after that Christmas Eve moment in the living room, whether she'd guessed at how he felt about her. Yet that moment had never repeated itself and she'd never said anything, so he'd told himself she hadn't guessed, and it was better that way.

Perhaps she hadn't. She did now, though.

He should have said nothing, should have let the moment pass unremarked. But he didn't.

'No,' he said fiercely instead. 'Don't look at me like that, Alice.'

Her eyes widened even further, the red blush staining her cheeks now creeping down her neck, and that was when he realised things were going to be even more complicated than they were already.

Because Alice felt the same way he did.

CHAPTER FIVE

ALICE'S HEART WAS beating so loud she was surprised it wasn't audible through the entire helicopter cabin, even despite the headset she wore.

He'd told her so fiercely not to look at him that she'd obeyed without even thinking about it, turning to look out of the window instead. Except she paid no attention to the Spanish countryside unrolling beneath them.

All she could think about was the moment when he'd looked into her eyes, and she'd seen something leap in the depths of his golden gaze. Something hot. Something that had felt like a caress of flame over her skin, searing her.

Once, she'd thought she'd seen something similar in his eyes a couple of years ago, on Christmas Eve. Everyone else had gone to bed and he'd disappeared down to the stables. She'd been alone. She'd stood in front of the fire, allowing herself to relax for the first time since she and Edward had arrived, because she never could, not in Sebastián's presence. She'd been thinking that perhaps this would be the last Christmas she and Edward would come to Spain, because it was getting too difficult for her. Emily had been asking her what was wrong and why was she so quiet, and, really, it would have been easier to stay at home. She could hardly tell her sister that it was because of Sebastián. Because his presence made her want things she shouldn't want.

Something had alerted her, as if the air pressure in the room had changed, and she'd glanced towards the doorway. And he'd been there, staring at her, the look on his face fierce with an expression she hadn't understood. His eyes had seemed to burn as golden as the flames in the grate and she'd felt herself catch fire along with them.

But then he'd turned away abruptly and left without a word. Afterwards, she'd told herself it was nothing. That perhaps he'd been looking for Emily and the expression she'd seen on his face was anger that he couldn't find her. Anger that it was Alice in the room instead of his wife.

Perhaps it's anger now.

Alice swallowed, her heart still beating far too loud. Their conversation had definitely been fraught and difficult and, yes, he was angry with her. But…the heat in his eyes hadn't been anger, she was certain. There had been an intensity to it that made her feel as if she were prey under the gaze of a starving wolf.

She shut her eyes and took a deep, soundless breath, trying to get her heartbeat under control. But that only made it worse, because it only made her more aware of his powerful, muscular body sitting next to hers and how tense he was, like a drawn bow just before the arrow was released.

Desperately she tried to think of something to say to ease the weight of the silence, but she couldn't think of a word. All she could think of was that look in his eyes. The look she'd dreamed of him giving her so many times, even though she knew it was wrong.

He was hungry for her. He wanted her. Maybe she'd imagined it back then on that snowy Christmas Eve. But she wasn't imagining it now.

It doesn't change things.

No, no, it couldn't. Neither of them was bound by marriage vows now, it was true, but he'd still been her sister's husband. And she'd been Edward's wife. She'd loved Edward once and, while he'd been unfaithful to her, she wouldn't use the excuse of his death to jump into bed with someone else only two months after he'd gone. Especially not when that someone was her own sister's husband. Edward might have not been able to control himself around Emily, but she'd been controlling herself around Sebastián for years and she wasn't about to stop doing so now. Also, if Sebastián himself had wanted to do anything about that hunger, he would have done so. At the very least he would have said something, but, since he hadn't, it was obvious that he wasn't about to take any action himself.

It didn't matter. It had never mattered. Neither of them had been in any position to act on their feelings before and they still weren't. There was Diego to consider after all.

Perhaps it would be better to simply ignore the moment as if it hadn't happened. Pretend that she hadn't seen the heat in his eyes, that he hadn't told her to stop looking at him like that.

As if you're just as starving as he is?

She forced the thought away. No, she wasn't starving. She didn't want him. It was better if she convinced herself of that because nothing was going to change between them. Nothing at all.

Slowly, Alice opened her eyes and risked a glance at the man sitting beside her. He had a sleek tablet in his hands and was doing something that must be very important because he was staring ferociously at it as if it were the most fascinating thing in the entire universe.

Her thoughts drifted back to what he'd told her about his father and about how he wasn't Mateo's biological son, that he'd been the product of his mother's affair with a stable hand. That little fact had got lost in the abrupt crackling heat that had sprung between them, but she couldn't forget it.

That had shocked her. It had also made his determination to claim Diego as his own far more understandable, since Diego was the product of an affair, too. Except Sebastián had been adamant that he wouldn't treat Diego the way his own father had treated him. He hadn't elaborated on what way that was, but, given how he'd brushed off her question, it probably wasn't good.

It made her curious, though, and she wanted to know more. But this wasn't the time for yet more difficult conversations, so she left him to whatever work he was doing, staying silent for the rest of the trip and staring out of the window. Trying to distract herself with plans for Diego and how she could find ways to keep herself in his life that wouldn't involve too many confrontations with Sebastián.

It wasn't until they came in to land on the rooftop of a beautiful old building in central Madrid that Alice realised she should have been thinking about more immediate concerns. Such as being in his presence for however long this business trip lasted and just how that was going to work.

As soon as the helicopter's rotors slowed, Sebastián got out, talking in rapid Spanish to a tall, older woman in a black uniform who was waiting on the rooftop. She glanced at Alice then back at Sebastián, nodding all the while. Then, without a backward glance, Sebastián walked away.

Okay, so that was how it was going to be. That was good. Distance was better for both of them.

Alice got out of the helicopter and the woman introduced herself in heavily accented Spanish as Gabriela, the duke's housekeeper, and said that he'd instructed her to show Alice around and to provide anything she might need.

Where the hacienda was full of old-world charm,

Sebastián's Madrid apartment was sleek and modern. Inside it was all white walls, black accents, and gold fittings. Gabriela showed Alice to a beautiful bedroom with long gauzy curtains covering the windows and wide white bed scattered with pillows and cushions. Then she asked Alice what she needed in the way of clothes and other 'comforts' since she hadn't brought anything with her.

Alice—uncharacteristically—hadn't remembered that until Gabriela mentioned it and abruptly became aware that she was standing in this beautiful, sleek-looking apartment that had probably cost millions and she was in old shorts and a T-shirt. And not only that, but she also hadn't brought her phone or any money, or even her passport.

She began to explain to Gabriela, but the older woman only shrugged, simply stating that since the duke had instructed that all her needs be met, they would be met. Clothes would be brought for her, as would anything else.

It was going to be difficult to refuse since she could hardly keep wearing her clothes for three days straight, and she had no money to buy any more. However, Alice did insist on finding her own clothes and that an itemised list of prices be kept so she could pay Sebastián back. Gabriela merely shrugged.

The afternoon was taken up with a visit to an incredibly high-end department store with Gabriela, who attended to all the payments. Alice tried to buy a few cheapish items, only to have hangers of beautiful dresses shoved at her by the very insistent housekeeper.

Again, she very much wanted to refuse, but since there was nothing to do in the apartment except sit, and since she was in Madrid and having dresses shoved at her, she might as well try them on, if only to keep herself amused.

Unfortunately it seemed that quite a few of them Gabriela insisted she buy, since 'the duke is paying' and then some matching shoes needed to be bought, also underwear of the lacy, silky variety. Then Alice found herself back in the apartment that evening, surrounded by bags and boxes and feeling a little like Cinderella.

Everything had been astonishingly expensive, and she was already trying to think of how she would pay for it all, and berating herself for spending so much money. Except she'd never had a shopping trip like it. Even when she and Emily would do a sisters' shopping trip, it had mostly ended up being about Emily buying lovely, delicate, feminine things, while nothing had seemed to fit Alice the way it fitted her sister. She always felt too tall, too large, too ungainly. An Amazon trying to fit into a dress made for a delicate fairy.

But she hadn't been able to resist the dresses that Gabriela had shown her, each one making her feel as if somehow some magic had been employed and she really was the fairy she'd always longed to be.

It was silly to indulge herself like that, not to mention pointless. Because where would she ever wear any of them? At home it was always suits to work and then sweat pants in the evening to sit in front of the TV. Even when Edward was alive, that was all she'd wear. He hadn't seemed to care, which had been nice on the one hand, but, on the other, he'd never mentioned it when she *had* made an effort, so it had also left her feeling unappreciated.

Gabriela hadn't mentioned when Sebastián would be back, which was annoying. She had to force this discussion with him somehow, get some kind of resolution, otherwise what would have been the point of coming to Madrid?

An idea stole through her head, one she'd never contemplated before and shouldn't be contemplating now and yet she couldn't shake it.

There was one way she could get his attention. One way to *make* him have this conversation with her. One way to bring him round to her way of thinking, even.

She could use the physical chemistry between them, the desire that flared whenever they were near each other. It was maybe a little manipulative, but this was Diego they were talking about and she'd do whatever she had to do for him.

Of course, there was always the risk of such a plan backfiring on her, but it wasn't as if she were going to sleep with Sebastián. She'd already decided that nothing would happen between them. She'd just… toy with him a little, cloud his judgement. It wasn't anything he hadn't been doing to her for the past five years, after all.

Feeling pleased with herself, she showered in the white marble and gold bathroom then carefully chose one of the dresses she'd bought, a beautiful deep red silk number with a plunging neckline and cut on the bias to enhance her curves, before falling from her hips to swirl provocatively around her thighs.

Then she went out to the huge open-plan dining/living area where she sat in grand solitude as Gabriela served her a delicious dinner of a tortilla and salad. No mention was made of when Sebastián would return, but that was fine. She'd just wait until he appeared.

Afterwards, Alice curled up with a book in one of the comfortable armchairs in the small library. On the low coffee table in front of her, Gabriela had put a glass of extraordinarily good Spanish red wine and some squares of chocolate.

It was nice to be looked after, Alice realised, and she could see why Emily had liked it so much. No thought was required and no energy expended. All she had to do was sit there and have all her needs catered for and for someone like her, who usually preferred to have control over most parts of her life, it was refreshing not to have to do it all herself.

She was just on the point of deciding whether she should have another piece of chocolate or a coffee to keep herself awake, when the door to the library opened and Sebastián walked in.

Instantly all thoughts of sleep vanished.

He stood in the doorway, darkly handsome, intensely attractive, with his tie loosened, the top buttons of his black business shirt undone, his golden eyes widening as he noticed her sitting there.

Her heart began to beat faster, harder, the air in the room getting as thick and electric as it had in the helicopter earlier on that day.

The approach she'd chosen for this conversation was dangerous, which meant she couldn't rush it. She had to do this carefully.

Taking a breath, she put down her wine and the book, slipping from the armchair and getting to her feet.

'Good, I'm glad you're back,' she said into the tense silence, hoping she didn't sound as breathless as she felt. 'We need to talk.'

He hadn't moved, his gaze searing as it scanned her from head to foot, following the curves of the red silk dress and then back up again. And there it was, once more, that hungry look in his eyes, the burning intensity that stole all the air from her lungs.

'Sebastián,' she managed, though what else she'd been going to say, she had no idea. Because that was the moment he finally moved towards her, striding forward as if for battle, as if nothing was going to stand in his way. And she should have done something, followed through with her plan, but she didn't. She stood there, her heart beating its way out of her chest as he stopped in front of her. Then he lifted his hands as if reaching for a prize he'd worked long and hard for, thrusting his fingers into her hair and dragging her head back. And his mouth covered hers and the whole universe stopped.

There was heat and demand and hunger. Years of aching need. Longing and desperation and she was lost to it. All her good intentions fell away, her plan and everything that went with it, all her guilt, all her grief. There was only his hard mouth on hers in a kiss that she'd spent so many years fantasising about, and now was finally happening.

She couldn't control herself. The thought of stopping simply didn't enter her head. Instead, she groaned in sheer relief and melted into him, winding her arms around his neck, leaning into the heat of his muscular body, opening her mouth, and letting him in. And he tasted as good as she'd always imagined he would. No, better. Like dark chocolate and Scotch, and everything delicious and sinful and wrong.

All of this was wrong and yet no power on earth would have pulled her away. His fingers were tight in her hair and he was devouring her as if he were starving. His tongue in her mouth, exploring, demanding, taking.

Then he shifted one hand from her hair down to the small of her back, pulling her hard against him, only the thin silk of her dress and the wool of his suit trousers separating them. She could feel the tensile strength of his body and it excited her. There was so much power there and he was so tall. Taller than Edward. Broader and more muscular, too. She loved that. Loved how it made her feel so delicate and feminine in comparison. She could feel the hard length of his arousal pressing between her thighs, his hunger for her obvious.

It thrilled her down to the bone.

She'd spent so long feeling unattractive and unwanted, and nothing she'd done to make herself more appealing had made any difference to Edward. He'd withdrawn from her so relentlessly and completely that eventually she'd stopped trying.

But now Sebastián wanted her. Sebastián was desperate for *her* and she wanted more than anything in the world to give herself to him.

The kiss went on and on, increasing in desperation until eventually Sebastián dropped one hand from her back and took a fistful of her dress, tugging hard and ripping the silk from her body. She barely noticed. Then she was on her back on the carpet in front of the small fireplace, and he was tearing at her underwear like a madman, shredding the flimsy material and getting rid of it.

His eyes glowed bright like coins, the expression on his beautiful face ferocious with desire. She grabbed at his tie, ripping it away then clawing at the buttons on his shirt, jerking it open to get to the hot skin beneath. She had dreamed of touching him for so long and she felt as if she might die if she didn't right this instant.

He gave a low masculine growl as her hands touched his chest, hot skin and crisp hair and hard muscle. Then he shifted, reaching down to jerk the buttons of his trousers open, shoving her thighs apart as he did so, pressing them wide, opening her up to him.

She was panting now, the pressure and the dragging ache between her legs becoming impossible to fight. The air around them was full of the sound of their panting breaths and then suddenly he was there, the long thick length of him pressing through the soft folds of her sex. Sliding into her so easily, so perfectly, just as she knew he would.

He was made for her. She felt it deep in her heart. In her soul.

She cried out as he settled inside her and arched up into him, the press of his body against hers, the weight of him on her so right. His fingers threaded through hers as he took her hands up and over her head, pressing them down to the carpet and holding them there. And he began to move, hard and deep, golden eyes staring down into hers as if transfixed.

There was fierce desire in them and also shock, as if he couldn't believe they were actually doing this, and she felt the same shock echoing through her.

They were joined finally and at last, and the sensations were indescribable. So much heat and need. Relief and a burgeoning wonder at what was happening. At how good it was to be here together, after so many years.

She wanted to say his name but she couldn't speak, the feelings becoming more and more intense with each passing moment. Her fingers tightened around his as she watched the pleasure glow in his eyes and knew he could see the same in hers. It was an endless feedback loop of ecstasy that only stoked the madness higher.

It didn't last. It couldn't. They'd held back for so long and she was only human.

The orgasm came crashing down on her with unstoppable force far too quickly and with far more power than she'd ever imagined, a wave of pleasure so intense that his name finally burst from her in a hoarse cry. Then he was moving faster and harder until he bent his head and covered her mouth again as it took him too.

Sebastián lay there, the silence broken only by their fractured breathing, for one long moment blissfully free of thought. Reality was the softness of the woman beneath him, the scent of sex and lavender in the air, and a physical contentment he couldn't recall ever feeling.

Then reality crashed in on him.

This was Alice. His sister-in-law. And he'd lost control. Spectacularly. All his good intentions, everything he'd told himself about restraint and being cold, being distant, had gone out of the window the moment he'd seen her curled up in the chair. In that red silk dress that made her sexy enough to tempt an angel.

And an angel he was not.

All day, in the endless meetings he'd attended with his bankers and lawyers, securing Diego's future, and setting in stone that this boy was his son and heir, when he should have been paying attention, he'd been thinking of Alice.

Thinking of that moment in the helicopter, when he'd known in an instant that she'd wanted him every bit as badly as he'd wanted her. But he'd decided that he would not act on it. Could not act on it. And every second of the day he'd told himself the same thing over and over, that desire was a bad thing, it led people down the wrong path. It hurt people. It made them mean and cruel and petty. It made them like his father, and he wouldn't allow that to happen to himself. He was better than that.

He'd purposely stayed later than he'd needed to with his lawyers, just to make doubly sure of his control, and when he'd finally got back to the apartment, he'd been looking forward to settling in the library with a glass of good Scotch.

Except she'd been there, curled in the chair. Her hair loose over her shoulders, wearing a red silk dress that clung to every one of her delectable curves. She'd looked up from the book she'd been reading, and her dark eyes had met his and the moment from the helicopter had rushed back in on him.

Then she'd got to her feet, the fabric of the dress swirling around her, outlining lush breasts and generous hips, and all he'd been able to think about was how much he wanted to rip that dress from her body and finally get his hands all over her. How impossible it was maintaining such control over himself

when she was right in front of him, and they were
both finally free.

How he couldn't bear it a second longer.

Every step he'd taken towards her had been a mistake, every action as he'd reached for her a grievous
error. They'd built on each other, all those mistakes,
until he'd been crushed by the weight of them and
then nothing had mattered any more.

To slide his fingers through the silken glory of her
hair and then feel the softness of her mouth open beneath his had been like finding water in the desert.
Such a profound relief. Then having her body press
against his… He'd never let himself fantasise about
it but the feel of her had been better than anything he
could have imagined.

He'd wanted to spend hours exploring her lush
body, but there hadn't been any time to spare. He'd
been too desperate. And when he'd spread her thighs
and finally slid inside her, becoming one with her, it
had felt like coming home.

You have made a mistake. A terrible mistake.

He didn't want the cold trickle of doubt to disturb
his contentment, but it did all the same, the trickle
becoming a flood.

He'd crossed the line he'd drawn for himself years
ago, broken the private vow he'd made never to treat
her as anything more than his sister-in-law. It didn't
matter that Emily had gone. It didn't matter that she'd
been unfaithful to him, and that they hadn't shared a

bed for over a year. It didn't matter that she'd fallen in love with someone else.

He'd promised himself he would never do anything about Alice, and he'd broken that promise. Now all those years of denying himself meant nothing.

Desire was a terrible force. It had driven Sebastián's mother into the affair that had eventually led to her having Sebastián and then dying. It had fuelled Mateo's jealous rage at being betrayed, which he'd then taken out on Sebastián.

And Sebastián's own desire to belong to someone had driven him to seek out the only man he'd ever felt a kinship with: Javier, who had managed the stables and who'd turned out to be Sebastian's biological father—not that he'd known that at the time.

Desire caused nothing but pain and he'd tried so hard to keep his own in check, but he'd failed. And it was too late to pretend it hadn't happened. Too late to go back and make a different choice.

You didn't even remember a condom.

Yet more ice slid down his spine.

He shifted, pushing himself away from Alice and getting to his feet, putting his clothes back in order. His hands were shaking.

'Sebastián?' Her voice was soft and husky and there was an uncertain note in it that tugged at his heart.

He gave himself a minute to gather the tattered remnants of his control then glanced at her.

She was sitting on the floor, her bra half off one shoulder, her knickers a scrap of ripped lace off to one side, her hair a black smoky storm. Her lips were red and full, and she looked thoroughly ravaged and so utterly beautiful he nearly lost control a second time and reached for her.

Instead, he said the first words that entered his head. 'I didn't use a condom.'

Colour crept through her cheeks, and she glanced away. 'It's fine. You don't need to worry about that.' Her voice had lost the uncertainty, becoming so determinedly neutral, he knew that somehow he'd hurt her.

Of course you hurt her. You took her like an animal and then the first words out of your mouth were about a lack of condom. Nothing about her. Nothing about how beautiful she was or how good she made you feel.

His chest tightened. She was reaching for the remains of her dress and trying to put it on, though it was now thoroughly ruined. Her hands were shaking too.

'Alice,' he said, trying to sound gentler. 'I should have found one—'

'I said, you don't have to worry about that.' She was looking at him now, and he could see a flicker of anger in her eyes.

'Why not?' he asked without thinking. 'Are you on the pill?'

She got to her feet, still clutching the remains of her dress around her, and lifted her chin. Her expression was shuttered and that made his chest tighten even more. 'No.' Her voice was as flat as his had been.

'You don't need to worry about that, because I can't have children, okay?'

He blinked in shock. 'What?'

'I'm not sure how much clearer I can be, Sebastián.' The red silk falling around her half-naked body and the oddly defiant look in her eyes made her look as regal as an empress. 'I had a bad miscarriage a couple of years ago and now I'm infertile. So don't worry, you won't be having any unexpected consequences from this little…mistake.'

She sounded cool and yet he knew now that she wasn't. He'd held her in his arms, been inside her, felt her passion join with his in a bonfire so bright and so hot it eclipsed the sun. He also knew that, no matter how expressionless or cool her voice sounded, the miscarriage had been the thing that had devastated her. Had dimmed that light inside her. And now he'd been thoughtless with a question he shouldn't have asked and it had hurt her. *He* had hurt her. And she didn't deserve that.

'Alice…' He took a breath, running a distracted hand through his hair. 'I had no idea…'

'Of course, you didn't. Why would you? No one knew except Edward.'

'Emily didn't—'

'No.'

'I'm sorry,' he said when she didn't say anything else. 'I didn't mean to hurt you.'

'I'm not hurt.' She tightened the fabric around her. 'Now, if you don't mind, I think I'll go to bed.'

She began to move past him, but his hand shot out before he was even conscious of it doing so, his fingers closing around her arm, her skin warm and silky beneath his fingertips. She stopped in her tracks, looking straight ahead. 'Sebastián, I don't—'

'We need to talk about what just happened,' he said shortly, because now he was starting to think straight again, they really did. He could, of course, pretend that this had never occurred. Simply ignore it and continue on with their lives, and yet how could they do that when they still had Diego to negotiate?

Her head turned, her dark gaze unreadable. 'Do we? It was a mistake, I think we can both agree, so what more needs to be said?'

'Was it really a mistake to you?' He shouldn't be asking her this, especially when he agreed. But he couldn't stop himself. Couldn't stop his fingers from tightening on her arm, because touching her bare skin was something he'd never get enough of.

She didn't look away, and he could see the embers of the heat between them, still smouldering, ready to burst into flame at any moment. But also hurt and regret and a thousand other things he couldn't interpret.

He felt the same way. It was so complicated, and he knew he shouldn't be pushing her, that it was dangerous. That if he wasn't careful and pushed too hard, he'd lose control of himself a second time and they'd end up where they had been not five minutes earlier. Naked on the floor. And that wouldn't solve anything.

'I...' She stopped then took a breath. 'Of course,

it was a mistake. How could it be anything else? It was the grief talking, that's all, and it shouldn't have happened.'

But it wasn't the grief, or maybe not *only* the grief. It had been more than that. When he'd looked down into her eyes as he'd been deep inside her, he'd seen the wonder there, glowing bright.

Except pretending this *thing* between them didn't exist was the lie they'd told themselves for years, the lie they kept on telling themselves in order for them both to have the future they wanted.

A future that had been destroyed by their respective spouses.

Now all they had were the remains: grief and guilt and no answer to either.

He shouldn't make this harder. He shouldn't want to hear her say that it hadn't been the grief, that it had been more, because there was nothing to be gained from that conversation. Knowing it wouldn't make the slightest bit of difference to the distance they had to keep between them.

Perhaps, after all, it was easier if they pretended nothing had happened.

Yes, that was probably for the best.

He dropped his hand from her arm, the warmth of her skin lingering on his fingertips. 'You're right,' he said. 'It was a mistake. I'll let you get to bed.'

Something flickered through her gaze, though he couldn't tell what, and then, without another word, she left the room, leaving him to the silence.

CHAPTER SIX

ALICE BARELY SLEPT. Every time she closed her eyes, she could see Sebastián's face in the darkness behind her lids. The carved lines of his features harsh and fierce with desire, pleasure glowing bright in his eyes. Pleasure that *she* gave him. And then everything he'd given her in return…

Her body pulsed with the reminder of the passion he'd poured into her. The way he'd ripped her dress away and her underwear too, as if he couldn't wait to get his hands on her. Then his kiss, the blinding heat of it…

Restlessly, she turned over in bed yet again, aching, unable to stop thinking, too, of the aftermath. After all of that wonder and pleasure the first words out of his mouth had been 'I didn't use a condom'. As if he hadn't shared any of that wonder and ecstasy with her. As if the only thing that had mattered to him was the possibility that she might be pregnant.

Perhaps she shouldn't have flung the truth of her miscarriage in his face, but it had felt as if he'd taken something special and precious and thrown it in the dirt. She'd felt a momentary sense of satisfaction at the look of shock on his face when she'd told him, and it had been enough to help her walk from the room with her head held high. But then that satisfaction had vanished and all she'd felt was sick guilt.

She'd showered before she'd gone to bed, even though part of her hadn't wanted to wash away the scent of him on her skin, desperate to hold onto the physical reminders for as long as she could.

But nothing could wash away what he'd said to her and how cheap she'd felt afterwards. Or the knowledge that he'd felt that same guilt too, because she'd seen it in his eyes.

The only way forward, it seemed, was to pretend it hadn't happened. They still had the situation with Diego to negotiate and she couldn't afford to let something as meaningless as sex get in the way of that.

You made a terrible, terrible mistake.

Alice turned over yet again. Yes, so she had made a mistake, but it needn't be catastrophic. If they pretended it hadn't happened, they could move on. They didn't have to let it get in the way of what they needed to do with Diego. It would be fine. In fact, it might even have been a good thing. Perhaps without the sexual tension in the air between them, their negotiations with Diego would go more smoothly.

It was a comforting thought, and yet still she didn't sleep.

Eventually, when the first light of dawn showed around the edges of the curtains, she hauled herself out of bed, gritty-eyed from lack of sleep. She grabbed a white robe from the bathroom and put it on, then went out into the kitchen in search of coffee. Only to find Sebastián already up and leaning against one of the kitchen counters, sipping an espresso.

And it wasn't until that moment that she realised it was going to be impossible to pretend the night before hadn't happened, that all the blazing sexual tension that had always been between them didn't exist. Because it did.

In fact, it seemed to have only increased, because seeing him standing there, dressed in a pair of worn jeans and a loose white shirt, his black hair damp from a recent shower, the shirt open at the neck to reveal the smooth brown skin of his throat… God. He was still just as gorgeous as he'd been the night before.

Now, though, it was even worse. Because now she knew what his mouth tasted like, and how hot his skin felt under her hands. That his eyes glowed bright when he was aroused and when he pushed inside her, it had felt as if he'd been made for her alone.

She didn't know what to do or what to say. The breath had been completely ripped out of her.

Sebastián didn't move as she met his gaze and her mouth dried, her heart once more galloping around in her chest the way it always did when he was near.

'Good,' he said. 'You're up. We need to talk.'

A little shock went through her, though she tried not to show it, resisting the urge to adjust her robe in a nervous movement. 'About Diego, I assume?' she asked with what she hoped was her normal cool.

'About Diego, yes.' He turned, put his cup down on the counter, then went over to one of the cupboards and took out another. 'Among other things.'

Her hands clenched into fists at her sides. 'What other things?'

Sebastián went to the stove and picked up the stove-top coffee maker, pouring some of the thick black liquid into the cup he was holding. Then he glanced at her, the look in the smoky gold of his eyes utterly unreadable. 'Milk?'

'I…uh…yes, please.'

He poured some milk into the cup from a small jug on the counter. 'Sugar?'

The electricity in the air was building again, the tension making her want to tear her skin off or scream, or do something equally inappropriate.

'What is this all about?' she asked instead, struggling to keep her voice even. 'And no, I don't take sugar.'

He came over to where she stood and held out the cup, and her mouth went even drier at his nearness. She could feel his warmth, smell his delicious scent— soap and that musky, masculine spice.

Her hand trembled slightly as she reached for the cup, the way he was watching her not helping. There was something intent in his eyes, something she didn't understand.

She took a desperate sip of the coffee, the hot,

strong hit of caffeine settling her nerves a little. 'Well?' she asked after a moment. 'Stop being so irritatingly mysterious and tell me what things you want to discuss.'

He folded his arms across his chest, seeming somehow even taller and broader than he had a second ago. The intensity in his eyes didn't falter.

He seemed…changed. Not angry the way he'd been before, more as if he'd made a decision that he was very, very certain about.

Her heart began to beat even faster.

'There is the matter of Diego, of course,' he said. 'But there is also the matter of you and me.'

Instantly her face heated, which was annoying in the extreme. 'Oh?' She hoped her voice sounded as cool as she wanted it to be. 'Weren't we going to pretend that didn't happen?'

'No. *You* were going to pretend it didn't happen.'

A strange panic filled her. 'But we both agreed that it was a mistake and we were—'

'I've changed my mind.' His eyes glinted in a way that made everything inside her contract.

'What do you mean you've changed your mind?'

The sharply carved lines of his face shifted, his hard mouth almost curving, as if he knew a secret she didn't. 'Drink your coffee. You're going to need it.'

The strange panic inside her began to gather momentum, though she didn't understand what she was panicking about. He was being deliberately vague and it was as annoying as hell.

'What are you talking about, Sebastián?' she demanded. 'Don't be so bloody aggravating.'

'I thought you'd prefer to be fully caffeinated before we have this discussion.' His voice was mild but that glint in his eye was anything but. 'You look like you haven't slept a wink.'

Alice gritted her teeth, trying to hang onto what little poise she had left. 'I slept fine,' she said shortly. 'Just tell me, for God's sake.'

'Drink your coffee.'

She wanted to refuse and perhaps throw his stupid coffee back in his face, but that would be to admit he was getting to her, and she didn't want to do that. He already had far too much power as it was. Besides, she was also desperate for the caffeine. So she downed the small cup in one go then held it up. 'There. I've had my coffee. Happy?'

His mouth curved again for reasons she couldn't guess at. He took the cup from her hand and placed it back on the counter. 'Emily always told me you were stubborn,' he said. 'That will make things…interesting.'

'What things?' Alice glared at him. 'Explain, please.'

'Very well.' He was all calm. 'You remember I told you yesterday that I wished to remarry, that Diego needs a mother?'

'Yes. What's that got to do with anything?'

He leaned back against the counter and folded his arms, his gaze very direct. 'How would you feel about becoming my wife?'

Shock rippled through her, and it was a good thing she wasn't still holding onto her coffee cup otherwise she would have dropped it. 'Be your wife? What?'

'As I said, Diego needs a mother and I need a wife. You want to keep Diego. Getting married would seem a logical solution to both our issues.'

The shock moved slowly outwards, making her stomach twist, and she was aware that beneath the shock, there was also an instinctive thrill of joy. As if being his wife was exactly what she wanted. Which it wasn't. At all. In fact, she was horrified by the suggestion.

'Are you insane?' She stared at him. 'I'm Emily's sister. And she's only two months dead.'

'I realise that. We can wait six months if you prefer.'

'You can't be serious.'

His jaw hardened. 'Oh, I am. Very serious. I want Diego to have a proper family and that includes a father and a mother. I would also like more children.'

Alice struggled to get hold of herself. 'I can't have more children. I told you that last night.'

He lifted one powerful shoulder. 'Not biological children, no, but you can certainly have children in other ways. As you can imagine, blood ties aren't much of a concern to me.'

Of course. He hadn't been his father's biological son, either, as he'd told her the day before. Interest once again flickered through her, belated questions crowding in her head, but since they were the least of her concerns right now, she ignored them.

'You don't need me for adoption,' she said. 'Or surrogacy.'

'The children will still need a mother,' he pointed out.

'What about Sofia? Or another nanny?' She'd told him earlier that Diego needed a mother, and he did, but panic was clouding her thinking.

'A nanny they will certainly have,' he interrupted, relentless. 'But a nanny is not the same as a mother.'

Of course, it wasn't.

Alice swallowed, the panicky feeling intensifying. She couldn't marry him. It was a ludicrous idea. She barely knew him. And she was only just a widow. Why would she rush into marrying someone else so soon, especially him? She didn't love him, and he certainly wasn't asking because he loved her.

'Why me?' she demanded. 'You could have any woman you wanted. It doesn't have to be me.'

He didn't even blink. 'I don't care much about blood ties, as I said, but you do. You're Diego's aunt, his only blood relative. You want to be in his life, yes?'

'I do, but—'

'If you and I are married, you can formally adopt him as your son. All the legal complications will be resolved. There is also one other reason it must be you.' He paused a moment, the intense light in his eyes glowing even brighter. 'I have no intention of divorcing you, and, since I will never be unfaithful, physical desire is vital.'

This time the shock that went through her was hot, making her face flame and her skin tighten. Making her very aware of the night before, of being in his arms, of screaming his name...

'Yes,' he murmured, watching her, reading every single one of her thoughts. 'That is why it must be you, Alice. You and only you.'

Sebastián could barely stop himself from reaching for her, but he managed it. Control at this delicate stage was of the utmost importance.

He knew this would be a shock to her and she needed time to come to terms with it, to think about it.

Marrying Alice...

The solution had come to him in the middle of the night, as he'd lain alone in his bed, every part of his body aching, tormented by thoughts of her and what had happened in that library. Him, losing control. Her, reaching for him, welcoming him. The feel of her better than any fantasy.

She'd wanted to pretend it had never happened and he'd agreed that it had been a mistake. Then he'd started thinking about having to negotiate potential custody issues with her and what they were going to do about it, and how he'd manage to keep resisting the temptation of her...

It had come to him in that moment that there was an answer to all his problems. *Their* problems. He'd known after Emily had died that he wanted to marry again, to give Diego a loving mother at his side.

Sebastián himself hadn't had one and, with nothing to soften Mateo's resentment or to provide even a loving counterpoint, it had been terribly lonely and isolating. And since neither he nor Javier, his biological father, had known of their relationship to each other, because Mateo had kept it secret, he'd felt as if he'd had no one at all to whom he'd truly belonged.

No, he wanted to make sure Diego never felt like that. That he grew up never knowing how painful love was. That he would be accepted, regardless of who he was. That he belonged.

Sebastián knew his own nature all too well, that his emotions were strong and had to be ruthlessly contained and controlled. Which meant Diego would need someone who didn't have to constantly hold themselves back and that someone would be Sebastián's wife. That person would be Alice.

You want her for yourself...don't use Diego as an excuse to justify it.

He was doing nothing of the kind. He knew the dangers of following his heart, of wanting things too desperately, and he kept his passions firmly confined. Yes, he'd lost control the night before, but making Alice his wife should take care of his physical desires. After all, what better solution was there? Alice was Diego's aunt and she wanted him, had been desperate enough to take on a legal challenge to have him. She would be the best mother for him. A lioness to protect him and love him, give him the family he deserved.

Yes, marrying her was the perfect fix for all their issues. Which meant the only issue left he had to deal with was Alice herself.

It was difficult to tell what she truly thought of the idea, because while she'd certainly been outraged, her face had also been flushed, and he could tell that she'd been thinking of the night before. She hadn't slept either—the dark circles under her eyes were proof enough of that.

Those beautiful eyes were very wide now and still full of shock and outrage. Yet not only that. The embers of the passion they'd shared last night were smouldering there too, banked coals just waiting to burst into life again.

It hadn't eased for her as it hadn't eased for him, either. One night would never be enough to satisfy his hunger and, after all, passion was allowed in marriage. He'd shared it with Emily, although he had to admit that what he'd experienced with Emily paled in comparison to what had happened between him and Alice.

You'd give Alice what you could never give to her sister? How is that fair?

But he wouldn't be giving Alice anything more than physical passion, so it was completely fair. His heart would never be involved. That wasn't what he wanted. Love was mean, it was punitive and demanding, and he was done with giving everything he had and it never being enough. Besides, Emily was gone now, and surely she'd forgive him spending physical passion with her sister. After all, she hadn't been faithful and it was too late now anyway. He'd crossed the line already.

'But I… I don't even know you,' Alice said faintly. 'Not really.'

'You know me. You've known me for five years.'

'No, I don't. I don't know the first thing about you. How could I? When you basically treated me as if I had the plague the whole time you and Emily were married.'

Irritation caught at him. While he'd expected her to be reluctant, after last night he'd thought she'd be more receptive to his proposal. Emily's and Edward's deaths were always going to be an obstacle, but still. It wasn't as if he and Alice were in love.

'Are you surprised?' he said shortly. 'It's not as if you welcomed me with open arms yourself.'

How can you say that? When it was you who held her at arm's length? You were cold and distant to her for a reason.

Her chin came up, the light of battle in her eyes, making the dark circles beneath them fade and warm colour stain her cheekbones. Even having no sleep and wrapped in a white robe, her hair tangled over her shoulders, she was so beautiful she stopped his heart. 'You've only got yourself to blame for that, Sebastián. I was ready to welcome you the day we first met. I couldn't wait to meet you, even. Then you looked at me as if I were dirt.'

He shouldn't admit to what he'd felt for her even back then. It felt wrong. A betrayal of the marriage he'd had with Emily. Yet if he wanted her to accept his proposal, he was going to have to give her the truth. He could see that now.

'Surely,' he said, 'you have some idea about why that was.'

She frowned. 'No, of course I didn't. Why would I?'

Perhaps she hadn't known. Perhaps she hadn't been completely conscious of the electricity that had been between them, what had always been between them. Or maybe she had been, but she hadn't understood what it was. Then again, could she have been that blind? Or that innocent?

Sebastián took a step closer to her. 'I think you do, Alice. I think you know damn well.'

Her cheeks had gone a deep red and he could see her struggle with the urge to step back and away from him, to put some distance between them. Yet she didn't move. She was a fighter, this woman. He liked that very much.

'So, you were attracted to me.' Her chin was held high. 'Is that what you're saying? That's why you were so cold and distant? For five years?'

There was accusation in her voice and admittedly it all sounded petty and ridiculous when she said it like that. Yet…he hadn't been able to do anything else. Not when he knew how susceptible he was to his own reckless heart.

He'd always been drawn to the stables, the gentle

acceptance of the horses soothing something in his wounded soul. Mateo had forbidden him to speak to any of the stable hands, but Javier, the stable manager, had watched him and noted his easy way with the animals, and had told him he had a gift. 'Come to the stables any time,' Javier had told him. 'I can teach you.'

Sebastián had been taught to ride by Mateo as soon as he could walk, but Mateo had been as harsh and exacting with him as he was with the animals. Javier had been different. He'd been gentler, kinder, intuitive and Sebastián had found him a much more knowledgeable and sympathetic teacher than his father had been.

He'd known it was wrong to talk to Javier; his father had forbidden it. But he'd been so desperate for a connection to someone, for attention that wasn't resentment and anger, that he hadn't been able to help himself.

Of course Mateo had found out, and when he had, he'd been furious. And he'd taken out his anger on Sebastián by telling him two secrets that he hadn't known, flinging them in his face like knives.

Firstly, that Javier was his biological father. And secondly, that he'd killed his own mother. She'd died having him.

Then he'd rounded out his vindictive tirade by firing Javier on the spot, then accusing Sebastian of being as faithless and disloyal as his mother and his biological father.

Sebastián had had no answer to that. He'd felt as if

his heart had been ripped from his chest, as if Mateo had simultaneously given him something precious before taking it back in the most brutal way possible. And later, in the furious aftermath of the confrontation, watching from his bedroom window as Javier had walked away from the job he'd loved, all he'd been able to feel was the most intense sense of failure. That he'd failed his mother, that he'd failed Javier. And somehow, he'd felt as if he'd failed Mateo too.

When Mateo had died years later, he'd picked up the mantle of the dukedom, determined to make up for his failures, and marrying Emily had felt as if he was firmly putting them in the past. Yet…he'd ended up failing her, too.

He'd given her everything she asked for, attention, physical pleasure, a house in Paris… Yet it still hadn't been enough.

You'd given your heart to Alice. You can't deny it.

No, this wasn't about his heart. His heart couldn't be trusted and he wouldn't listen to it, not again.

'It wasn't mere attraction,' he said, because attraction was too tame a word for the physical hunger he felt for her. 'It was almost obsession, Alice. And you know it. You felt it too. Or was there some other reason that you never let yourself be alone in the same room with me?' The red in her cheeks deepened, her eyes getting darker, and he stared at her, searching her face. 'Or were you afraid of me? Perhaps it was that? Did you think I would do something to you that you wouldn't want?'

'No,' she said quickly. 'No, of course not.'

He knew that wasn't it already. She'd never been afraid of him, only of the electricity between them, but he wanted her to say it. 'I couldn't get close to you, Alice. You must have known that. And I think you couldn't get close to me for the same reasons.'

She glanced away. The pulse at the base of her throat raced and he was close enough to feel her warmth. She smelled of lavender and sex and, though he wasn't even touching her, he was hard. But he'd already decided one thing: the next move was hers. He'd crossed the line the night before and she'd welcomed him. But now he needed it to be her turn. If this was to work, she had to show that she wanted him every bit as badly as he wanted her.

'I didn't… I never…' She stopped, her fingers fussing with the tie of her robe. Then she looked back at him, her gaze fierce. 'I was faithful to Edward. I always have been.'

'I wasn't implying otherwise. And I have always been faithful to Emily. But you changed everything. You must have known that.' He saw the admission in her eyes. It *had* changed for her too. 'Say it, Alice. I want you to say it. Out loud so I can hear it.'

He took a step even closer, so there were only inches between them. She wasn't as petite as Emily and he didn't have to look down as far. She didn't give off that air of fragility either, the delicacy that Emily had that he'd been so afraid of breaking. He could feel himself get even harder. Sometimes Emily had found his physical passion too much and, certainly in the last year, she'd kept putting him off. Kept telling him she had a headache, that she wasn't 'feeling it', that she was too tired.

But last night Alice had put her hands on him, and she'd been so hungry. He'd almost forgotten what it was like to have a woman desperate for him and he wanted more. He needed it. He wanted a woman whose passion matched his own and the night before Alice had certainly done that. Her body had been all luscious curves and soft skin. A feast he could spend days devouring.

She stared at him for a long moment, and he could see fear in her eyes. She was afraid of admitting what she felt, afraid of admitting what she wanted.

Well, he wasn't going to help her. She either wanted him, wanted this, or she didn't. There was no middle ground. And he wasn't going to force her into an admission. She had to choose it for herself.

'Edward's dead,' she said. 'It's been two months, Sebastián. Just two months.'

'Oh, I understand, believe me. I know all too well how many months it's been. But if you hadn't felt as I did, you wouldn't have reached for me last night the way you did. You wouldn't have kissed me back, and you certainly wouldn't have spread your legs for me so desperately.'

Her jaw hardened, anger leaping in her eyes. 'I would never have—'

'They're both dead, Alice,' he interrupted. 'You don't have to pretend any more.'

Her mouth opened then shut and she swallowed. Took a breath.

Then, before he could move, she reached for him.

CHAPTER SEVEN

HE WAS RIGHT. Even now, despite last night, she was still pretending.

Pretending she didn't want him with every breath in her. Pretending she wasn't desperate to touch him, to taste him. Pretending his physical presence didn't spin her world entirely on its axis.

Pretending had become such a deeply ingrained habit, though, that it was difficult to break. Difficult even to say the words out loud.

You're not alone, though. He always wanted you too.

All this time. From the moment he first saw her. It seemed impossible. He'd been so cold, so distant, and she'd thought the electricity in the air that always seemed to hover around them was only on her side. There had been times where it had felt as if he might feel the same way, that last Christmas Eve they'd all had, for example. But he'd never said anything. Never given her any reason to think that he even liked her, let alone wanted her.

But he had. And last night he'd proved it.

Now, in the kitchen, he was so close, his body hot, and the scent of him irresistible, and she had no idea what to do with his marriage proposal, no idea at all. It was so complicated. The prospect scared her, filled her with guilt and yet at the same time there was also a traitorous joy, as if being his wife was all she'd ever wanted to be.

It seemed easier to reach for him, touch him. Kiss him. Because the only thing that made any sense was the need inside her. That, at least, was simple.

Yet when she lifted her hands to him, his fingers closed around her wrists, holding her at bay, his golden eyes blazing.

'No, Alice,' he said softly. 'Give me the words. I want to hear you say them. You won't get anything until you do.'

She took a shuddering breath. His grip was unbreakable, the force of his will in every line of him. He wasn't going to move until she gave him what he asked for, that was clear. Which meant if she wanted him, she was going to say it, out loud.

Yet even now it still felt dangerous to admit, almost a transgression even though both Edward and Emily were gone, and she was betraying nothing but their memories.

They found each other. Why can't you and Sebastián?

Except Emily and Edward had clearly been in love, and she was not in love with Sebastián. Just as he was not in love with her. And she didn't want him to be.

She wasn't ready for love again, not after what her marriage had turned into, and, in fact, she might not ever be ready. Love was far too demanding and required so much, and she didn't have it in her to give anyone that except her nephew. But desire, passion... those she could do.

You need this. You need him. You need to be wanted.

Her heart ached. She did need it. In fact, she couldn't recall the last time anyone had wanted her the way Sebastián did. His desire healed something painful inside her.

'Well?' he prompted. 'Are you going to say it?'

Her mouth had gone dry at the fierce look in his eyes, her skin burning where he clasped her wrists in a strong grip. He'd given her the truth, surely she could do no less?

'I...want you, Sebastián,' she said huskily, the words feeling forbidden in her mouth and yet also so very right.

The glow in his eyes became brighter. 'How long, Alice? How long have you wanted me?'

She swallowed and gave him this truth too. 'Since I first saw you. When Emily first introduced us.'

His hard mouth curved slightly, but there was no amusement in the smile. Only an intense and very male satisfaction. He released her hands, but didn't otherwise move. He was waiting for her, that was obvious.

It wasn't a choice. Nothing was going to stop her from reaching to take his face between her palms the way she'd wanted to from the moment she'd walked into the kitchen. From relishing his hot skin and the prickle of his morning beard. From staring into his eyes and loving how he stared right back, and the relief that they could do this. That there was no reason to hide any more.

Then she went up onto her toes to press her lips to his. He didn't stop her this time, his mouth opening to greet her, and then the heat between them burst into flames, the feverish intensity leaping high as he took charge and utterly devoured her.

She loved it. She pushed her palms flat to the hard wall of his chest and kissed him back just as feverishly, just as hungrily, and just as demanding as he was.

Her fingers dropped to the buttons of his shirt, pulling them open so she could touch his bare skin, and then she was stroking him, feeling the iron-hard bands of his muscles flex and release as she traced them. He growled something against her mouth and the rough timbre of his voice thrilled her. Edward had been so unmoved by everything she did that she'd begun to doubt everything about herself, worried that she'd lost her attractiveness along with her fertility.

Yet that was patently not the case with Sebastián. He took her hands and pushed them down to the buttons of his fly, holding her palm against the denim. She could feel him, long and hard for her, making the pulsing ache between her thighs sharp and needy.

He said something rough and demanding in Spanish, but she didn't need any translation. She knew what he wanted.

She gave him a little push back so she had some space, then she dropped to her knees in front of him. It had been a long time since she'd done this—Edward hadn't enjoyed it, or at least that was what he'd told her—and she hadn't insisted. Her sexual confidence had taken a beating after losing the baby and Edward's withdrawal hadn't helped. But...here, now, Sebastián wanted her. He was on fire for her and he wanted to know if she was on fire for him, too.

Well, she'd show him. She'd prove it to him.

With shaking fingers, she pulled open the buttons of his jeans and released him. He murmured something in his deep voice, his fingers sliding into her hair, caressing. She didn't hesitate, gripping him, stroking velvety hot skin and steel, then opening her mouth and taking him in. He tensed, a low growl escaping him. His fingers flexed and tightened in her hair as she took him deeper.

'Alice,' he murmured, her name sounding like music in his accent. *'Mi cielo...'*

She had no idea what that meant, but she knew it was an endearment of some kind and it wound through her, a thread of gold gilding everything inside her. Edward had never called her anything but Alice, even when they'd first started dating. No sweetheart. No honey. No darling. Not even my love. Just Alice. Plain old Alice.

But then even that thought vanished as she tasted

him, loving the sounds she brought from him as his hips flexed and he drove himself into her mouth. She lost herself in that moment. Lost herself to the pleasure she gave him and when he made a low, guttural sound of release, it was her turn to take everything he gave her, and she did.

When he was done, he gave them a few moments then pulled her up and lifted her onto the kitchen counter, so she was sitting on it. He reached for the tie of her robe, tugging at it so the edges of the fabric parted. Then he slid one hand in her hair, pulling her head gently back, and he bent, covering her mouth with his.

Alice shuddered. He tasted of dark coffee and sin and when she leaned into his lips, kissing back hungrily, he made another of those low, masculine sounds that thrilled her so much.

'Slow down,' he murmured against her lips. 'We have plenty of time.' Then he slipped a hand between the parted folds of her robe, his touch a flame on her bare skin, and his kiss became slower, deeper, more intent. His fingers spread, cupping her breast in his palm, his thumb stroking over her hardened nipple, sending waves of shocking pleasure through her.

It felt so good. She couldn't speak, couldn't think. There was only his stroking hand moving over her skin, touching her, tracing her with such care it was as if he was committing every inch of her to memory.

Edward hadn't touched her that way, not even the first time they'd slept together. He'd been attentive, but he hadn't touched her as if she was rare and precious. As if he'd been dreaming of the feel of her skin for years and years.

But Sebastián did. Every caress of his fingers layering pleasure upon pleasure, until she was trembling with the force of it. His mouth had found its way to her throat, tasting the frantic race of her pulse, his hand dropping down between her thighs, stroking and teasing the soft flesh there with such lightness she could barely stand it.

'Oh, my God,' she whispered, her head tilting back, her eyes closing. 'Oh…please…'

'What do you want, *mi cielo*?' His voice was dark and deep as his fingers stroked over the sensitive part of her, making her shudder and shake. 'Tell me.'

She had her hands on his powerful shoulders, her fingertips digging in, her hips lifting against the movement of his hand. 'You.' She had to fight to get the words out. 'I want you.'

'Then look at me,' he ordered roughly.

She opened her eyes, obeying him without question, and there he was standing in front of her, his gaze full of a desire and a possessiveness that stole her breath. He pulled her to the edge of the counter, his fingers pressing hard against her flesh, and her thighs automatically parted to let him stand between them.

He stared at her so fiercely and kept on staring as he pushed inside her, long and slow and deep. She groaned, her whole body trembling, unable to look away from him, his golden eyes inches from hers. It was intensely intimate, as if he could see inside her head and she could see inside his. And he didn't flinch from her stare either. He let her see the fierce passion inside him and how it blazed, and all she could think about was how wrong Emily had been. Because he wasn't cold or distant. No, he burned like the sun. She could barely look at him.

Did Emily make him burn like this? Or is it all you?

But she couldn't think about her sister, not now, not like this. There was no room for Emily. There was only her and Sebastián as he began to move, holding her tightly, the rhythm a dance and both of them in perfect time.

It had never been like this with Edward. Never ever.

The pleasure built and built until there was no keeping it inside and the moment it exploded through both of them, he leaned forward and took her mouth. They shuddered and shook together, the flames consuming both of them.

They remained like that for long moments, locked together, his powerful body pressed to hers, his large, warm hands spread on her hips. She couldn't stop shaking with the aftershocks, the thought of him letting her go almost unbearable.

Finally, an eon later, he lifted his mouth from hers and pressed leisurely kisses along her jaw and down the side of her neck, his hands moving slowly over her hips and thighs, not inciting this time, but soothing.

'Well?' His deep voice was rough and frayed as worn velvet. 'Are you going to marry me, Alice?'

It must have been the effect of the orgasm, she thought later. Or maybe she was simply sick of fighting, and this seemed to be the easiest solution to a very complicated problem. Because all she could think about was that yes, she would marry him. If he could make her feel like this every day, despite the guilt, it would be worth it.

'Yes,' she said thickly. 'Yes, Sebastián, I'll marry you.'

He shouldn't have felt so satisfied at her quiet 'yes' but he did. Maybe it was no wonder. She'd knelt for him, taken him into her mouth, made him feel like a god, and it had been such a long time since he'd felt that way. A very, *very* long time.

It wasn't that Emily hadn't wanted him—she had. At least initially. Yet she hadn't much enjoyed his rougher, earthier passions, and had made that clear, so he'd got into the habit of restraining himself with her.

Then, later, Emily had slowly withdrawn from him, radiating a hurt she wouldn't admit to and that he couldn't seem to do anything about.

They'd taken to sleeping in separate rooms, because she'd claimed she slept better on her own, but he'd known it was more than that. It was him. It was his inability to give her what she'd wanted: love. He couldn't blame her for finding that with Edward.

The failure had always been his and he couldn't forget that.

Perhaps you will fail Alice too?

No, it would be different with Alice, because he wouldn't promise her anything he couldn't give. And he'd be completely up front about it so there'd be no misunderstandings, no pressure. A legal partnership and a family for Diego, and sharing a bed to satisfy their physical obsession with each other. That was all. It didn't have to mean anything more than that. It didn't have to be complicated.

He shifted, sliding his hands to cup her backside and pulling her even closer against him. She was so warm and she smelled of sex, and he was hardening yet again. He still felt as if he was starving for her and was already desperate to take her to bed yet again, but first, he needed to be absolutely clear on what the rules were for this situation so there would be no mistakes.

Her chin lifted as he gripped her, her dark eyes meeting his. There was uncertainty in them, but she didn't try to hide it. 'I can't help but think you've just manipulated me into saying yes using sex.'

He almost smiled. Things were going to be interesting in his household, since it was apparent that she wasn't going to shy away from difficult subjects. A refreshing change from Emily, who always had.

'That goes both ways, you know.'

'True.' She relaxed into him in a way that made him want to growl with possessive satisfaction. 'Okay, so how is this going to work? We're going to have to wait six months, because I don't want any commentary on how quickly it's all happening between us.'

'We don't have to make a performance of it,' he said,

relishing the feel of her bare skin against his palms. 'We can get quietly and legally married at a register office. My parents are dead, so are yours, who needs to know?'

She nodded slowly. 'I suppose I'll have to live with you, then?'

'If you want to give Diego the family he needs, then yes.' He paused a moment then added, because he wanted to acknowledge the fact that she would have to be the one shifting countries, 'I'm sorry, but I can't move to New Zealand. My place is here, on my estate. And I can't move the business either. But I'll buy you a house in Auckland that you can visit whenever you like.'

Again, she nodded, her expression thoughtful. 'I have an investment company, you know that. I don't want to give it up.'

'I would never ask you to. Could you work remotely?'

'Yes, I think I could do something like that.' She paused. 'What about the rest?'

He didn't need to ask what she was talking about. 'You'll live with me at the hacienda. You can have your own room if you want the space and you can live your own life however you choose. But at night you will sleep with me, yes? I won't have a sexless marriage, Alice. And I will be the only man you sleep with.'

This time a flicker of her temper glinted in her

eyes. 'You say that like I'm immediately going to go out and sleep with lots of men.'

And he could feel it growing inside him, a certain electric excitement at the thought of having her. Of *finally* having her. In his bed, in his house, in his life. Of having her whenever he wanted her, no need to hide, no need to control himself either. Sure, it was about sex, but he'd also appreciate getting to know her a bit more in a way he hadn't been able to before. She was such a passionate spirit. He couldn't wait to match wits with her. And anyway, shouldn't he know the woman who would be Diego's mother and his wife?

Are you sure that's a good idea? This has the potential to become something more if you're not careful.

No, it wouldn't. Because he *was* careful. He'd always kept his heart guarded and that wouldn't change just because she was in his bed.

'You'd better not,' he murmured, unable to resist teasing her. 'I could get quite unhappy if you did.'

Some of the anger in her eyes eased as she caught his tone, the tension around her mouth relaxing. 'Seriously, though. Have *you* really thought this through? What if we get to the point where we're not attracted to each other any more?'

He squeezed her a little, making her gasp and shiver. 'It's lasted for five years so far. I can't see it getting less any time soon.'

She slipped her hands into his open shirt, sliding her fingers over the bare skin of his chest. 'Perhaps it won't be as exciting if we no longer have to worry about other people.'

He knew what she was doing. She was trying to find excuses, voicing her fears. 'What are you worried about?' he asked. 'That I'll stop wanting you?'

Her stroking fingers paused, her gaze flickering away. 'It happens.'

It did and it had happened to both of them.

'This is about Edward, isn't it?' he asked.

She shifted restlessly, her hands dropping from his chest, but he caught them before they did, pressing her palms to his skin and holding them there.

'Tell me,' he said, because he was tired of not knowing, tired of her being such a mystery to him when all he wanted to know was more. 'Remember, it happened to me also.'

She sighed. 'Yes, it's Edward. After I lost the baby he…withdrew from me. And we…we didn't…' She stopped, a thread of pain in her voice. 'He didn't want me any more.'

Gently, Sebastián reached for a lock of her silky black hair and tucked it behind her ear. 'I can't tell you what was missing for Edward, but I can tell you that the fault wasn't with you. I have wanted you for five years, Alice. And like I said, I don't see that changing any time soon.'

Colour bloomed in her pretty olive skin, deepening the post-orgasmic flush already there, and he watched it, mesmerised. 'They were childhood sweethearts,' she said softly. 'He and Emily. We were all friends at school and I was in love with him for years as a teen-ager. I never thought he'd choose me. But for some reason, after high school he did, and I was so…happy. Except… I suppose I was always his second choice. He never fully moved on from her, did he?'

Sebastián had been aware of Emily and Edward's history, but he'd never suspected that Emily still had feelings for Edward. It was only after the accident that he'd realised.

'Did you love him?' he asked, unable to stop the flicker of a jealousy he shouldn't be feeling, not when he wasn't in love with Alice, and Edward was dead and gone.

'I thought I did,' she said. 'He didn't love me, though, that was clear.'

That had hurt her deeply, he could see it in her eyes, and of course it must.

'He was an idiot,' Sebastián said bluntly, because she had to know that was the case. 'And if he didn't see or appreciate what he had in you then he didn't deserve you, either.'

'He was always very respectful, very gentle. He was nice to me, so I don't—'

'*Nice?*' he demanded, oddly angry for reasons he couldn't have explained. 'If he wasn't at your feet worshipping you or spending all night feasting on your body because he couldn't get enough, then he was a fool. If the best you can say about him is that he was nice to you, then your marriage was doomed from the start.'

Alice's eyes widened, shock flickering in them, before that gave way to the familiar glitter of sparks. Her mouth opened, but he found himself saying, before she could, 'Don't defend him. If all he could give you was half-hearted caring and gentleness and *niceness*, then he shouldn't have married you. I have no respect for a man who squandered what he had.'

Says the man who did the same with his own wife.

Guilt ate at him, but he shoved it away.

Again, Alice's chin came up, her temper flaring. 'Are you going to give me more, then?' she demanded. 'Is that what I can expect from you?'

He gripped her tighter. There were things she couldn't expect from him, it was true, but at least he was honest about that. And he wouldn't be a hypocrite. He'd do better with her than he had with Emily. He'd certainly *never* make her feel as if she was anyone's second choice. 'I will *never* squander what I have in you,' he said fiercely. 'I will respect you, care for you, desire you. I will do everything I can not to hurt you. The only thing I can't give you is love, Alice.'

Emotions flickered through her gaze, though what they were he couldn't tell. 'Don't worry,' she said, her voice very neutral. 'In fact, it'll be a long time before I'm ready to love anyone again anyway. I'll settle for what you can give me.'

The word 'anyone' caught at him, as did the word 'settle'. A scrape against his skin and oddly painful. He ignored the sensation. 'If you do happen to fall in love with someone, we can discuss it. I don't want a divorce, but I'm sure we can come to some arrangements if need be.'

Her gaze suddenly became sharper, focusing on him in a way that wasn't comfortable. 'What about you? What if you fall in love with someone?'

'I won't.' He said it with the utmost certainty, because that was the last thing he'd ever do. 'Any love I have to give will go to Diego and that's all.'

'You didn't love Emily, then?'

The question sounded like an accusation, but then he supposed that was fair since he'd asked her the same thing about Edward.

'I tried to,' he said slowly, and he'd thought he'd managed it until Alice had come on the scene. 'But trying wasn't enough in the end.'

The sharp focus faded from her eyes, replaced with something like sympathy. 'No,' she murmured, regret in her voice. 'It never is, is it?'

She wasn't wrong. Love was never enough for anyone, or at least his wasn't. Not for his mother, not for his father, and not for Emily. Only the horses accepted his and didn't require anything more.

Part of him wanted to know why she thought the same and what had happened in her family to make her think so, because it wasn't just about Edward. Yet, another part of him was done with talking, especially when there were better things to be doing.

'Any other questions?' he asked abruptly. 'I'm hungry and not for breakfast.'

She didn't answer. Instead, she slid her arms around his neck and kissed him. And there was no more talking for a very long time.

CHAPTER EIGHT

TWO WEEKS LATER, Alice sat in the cool of the hacienda's courtyard, under the shade of the bougainvillea, Diego nestled in the crook of her arm. She'd just given him a feed and he'd settled down happily. He was such a good baby.

Alice felt much more comfortable with him now and it eased something in her heart just to sit here like this, in the heat of a Spanish summer with her nephew sleeping peacefully in her arms.

Pity the rest of it isn't so peaceful.

That was an understatement.

In the two weeks since they'd got back from Madrid, Sebastián hadn't wasted any time. He'd taken her to Seville where they'd got married in a quick register office ceremony. She'd felt uncomfortable marking the occasion in any way since it was only a purely legal affair, but had decided at the last minute to wear one of the dresses she'd bought in Madrid, a deep blue silk number that flattered her skin and her figure. She'd wondered initially what the point of wearing the dress was and then seen gold flare in Sebastián's gaze the second he'd laid eyes on her and knew then that *that* had been the point.

The ceremony had been quick and before she knew it, she was Sebastián's wife. Lucia had then cooked them a special dinner that night and they'd eaten only half of it when Sebastián finally lost patience, pushed his plate aside, pulled her up from her chair and took her to bed.

That was the only part of their relationship that seemed to function on any level. At night they explored each other, learned each other. She found out what he liked and, as it turned out, he liked everything and there was nothing about his body that was off limits to her. She gave him back the same, which he took full advantage of, learning all the things that gave her pleasure and then showing her new ways to experience it. She lived for their nights together.

During the day, though, it was a different story. He was almost a stranger to her, spending most of his time in his office or down in the stables. Mornings and evenings he reserved for Diego and she loved watching him with the baby, seeing him all patient, gentle, and caring. Protective too.

It made her hungry for him, made her want more of him, though she knew that the nights they spent together should be enough. She was almost shocked to find herself a little envious of her nephew, wishing that Sebastián were that way with her, which was ridiculous. She didn't want him to be. He'd been very clear in Madrid that their marriage would be only a physical and legal one, no emotions would be involved, and she'd agreed to it. She couldn't say she hadn't known what she was getting into when she'd said yes to his proposal.

She tried to ignore the feelings though and it was easy at first, since she was busy dealing with transferring her life from Auckland to Spain. She had help from Sebastian's staff, though she knew she was eventually going to have to go back to Auckland to deal with some of the practicalities herself. In the meantime, she'd decided to take a couple of weeks off to spend them as she'd originally planned, getting to know Diego and recovering from Edward and Emily's sudden loss.

Sofia came out to take Diego to put him down for his afternoon nap and, afterwards, Alice sat there in the quiet, listening to the cicadas, knowing she had a mile-long to-do list and that she'd better get onto it, and yet not moving.

It was always like this after Diego was asleep and there were things to do and yet she didn't do any of them. She couldn't stop thinking about Sebastián. About whether this was going to be her life now, living with the stranger who was her husband, about whom she knew very little. Each of them with their separate lives and meeting only at night, in bed, where their hunger for each other remained fierce.

It seemed ridiculous that she knew his favourite sex positions, yet she didn't know how he liked his coffee or whether he preferred movies to books, or what he'd wanted to grow up to be when he was a child.

Remind you of anything?

Alice shifted uncomfortably in her chair then leaned forward to stir her cold tea yet again. She didn't want to be thinking of Edward right now, but she couldn't deny the similarities. They'd stopped talking to each other in the year before he died, becoming virtual strangers to each other, and she hadn't known how to bridge the gap she'd sensed opening up between them.

It had been lonely, and she'd been so unhappy.

And now you're heading down the same path with Sebastián.

Yes, and if she wasn't careful, she was going to end up having the same life and the same marriage that she'd had with Edward. Only with Sebastián it would be worse, because while she had some of him at night when they were together, she didn't have the whole. Not that she was asking for the whole, but she'd like a lot more than what she had now.

Emily had found living in the hacienda isolating and lonely, Alice remembered, and now she knew why. Because if this was how Sebastián had treated her, no wonder she'd been lonely.

You agreed to the marriage. You knew what you were getting into.

Sadly, true. Emily had solved her issues by staying in the apartment Sebastián had bought her in Paris and then, of course, by having an affair with Edward. But then Emily had always wanted to be chased. Alice was different. She already knew no one was going to chase her and if she wanted to solve this problem, she was going to have to sort it out herself. Clearly Sebastián wasn't going to.

Edward had never wanted to talk, he'd brushed her off every time she'd tried to discuss what was happening in their marriage. And she hadn't pushed. She'd been afraid he'd simply decide she was too much trouble and leave.

She had that same fear with Sebastián. They didn't love each other. Also, he'd made his position clear. He didn't do divorce and he would never be unfaithful, and she believed him. He was very much a man of his word and had strong convictions, and she was certain he wouldn't just up and leave if she pushed him.

Deciding that sitting around thinking about it wasn't going to solve the issue any faster, Alice shoved her chair back and got up, making her way through the gardens to the stables.

Sebastián was with one of the mares, standing outside her stall and talking to Tomas, the stable manager. The mare had her head over the gate and was nuzzling at Sebastián's shoulder. As Alice watched, he lifted an absent hand and gave her long nose a stroke.

Alice shivered, a prickling excitement settling down low in her belly. He was so affectionate with the horses. That was what she'd been drawn to when she'd used to come down here initially, his gentleness and kindness with them so at odds with how cold he was to her. How they would come to him as if they knew he was someone they could love and trust.

She'd never had that, she realised with a sudden lurch. Even with Edward. Emily had been his first love and even though he'd chosen Alice, she'd always wondered if he'd regretted it. If she'd merely been a poor second choice. That doubt had lingered and she'd never been able to shake it. Especially after the miscarriage, as he'd withdrawn from her even more, taking her trust in him along with it.

Of course he regretted it. Why do you think he went and had a child with your sister?

Emily had always been the first choice, the better choice. Even when Alice had been a kid, her parents had prioritised Emily's appointments and play dates, school performances and sports days, and sometimes they forgot about hers. She could never trust that they would think of her first. She'd asked her mother once why that was, and her mother had replied that Alice could look after herself. Emily simply needed more than she did. And it was the truth. Emily always did.

Even now, though, you're not Sebastián's first choice.

No, but she didn't need to be. He, at least, had been honest with her about what he could give and what he couldn't, and, to be fair to him, he'd given her exactly what he'd promised. He'd certainly gone a long way to healing the hurt Edward had dealt to her physical and sexual confidence, so there was that. And as to more, maybe that would come in time.

What about love?

Perhaps she'd find love with someone else at some point. Or maybe this would be enough for her. Somewhere inside her something went stiff with denial at the thought, but she ignored it.

Instead, she waited until Sebastián had finished speaking with Tomas then, after the other man had left, she walked slowly over to the stall.

Sebastián eyed her, his expression guarded. 'Alice? Did you need something?'

Her heart was beating a little too fast, though she wasn't sure why since all he could do was refuse to talk to her and she didn't think he'd do that.

You want more from him than a mere 'talk'.

She ignored that thought too.

He was gorgeous today in casual jeans and a T-shirt that showed off his magnificent physique, and she found it difficult to concentrate on what she wanted to say. It seemed unfair that even after two weeks of gorging herself on him every night, she still struggled to string words together in his presence.

'I think we need to talk,' she finally managed.

He lifted one black brow. 'Talk? Talk about what?'

Alice took a steadying breath and folded her arms over her thundering heart. 'Our marriage, Sebastián.'

His expression betrayed nothing. 'What about it?'

'It's just… Is this how it's going to be from now on? You and I living completely separate lives except at night?'

He frowned. 'I'm not sure quite what the issue is. That's what I told you would happen, and you agreed.'

'Yes, I did. I just didn't realise I was expected to live here and be happy with you completely ignoring me.'

The mare nickered and nudged at his shoulder, and he reached up once more to stroke her nose. His gaze was dispassionate as he stared at her, and Alice was reminded yet again of what Emily had said about him seeming to care more for the horses than for her. Perhaps he did. Why that thought should feel so very disappointing she didn't know.

Are you sure you don't know? You want him to care for you and you always have.

No, she didn't want that. Why would she? She'd already been in love with one husband who'd seemed indifferent to her and she didn't want to fall for another. Sebastián wasn't indifferent at least, but she knew that was all about their physical chemistry, despite what he'd said back in Madrid about it being more than that. If it had been more, he wouldn't have distanced her, so clearly he'd been mistaken.

'You can live somewhere else if you'd prefer,' he said. 'You're not a prisoner here, Alice. You can go wherever you like.'

The inexplicable disappointment deepened into hurt. So not only did he not want to talk to her, he was also completely happy for her to leave.

He told you what to expect.

A physical marriage, that was all. And back in Madrid, on a high from the sex they'd had, she'd been fine with that. But now the reality of her situation was becoming apparent, she realised that actually she wasn't fine with that.

But there was no point in telling him she was hurt or making a fuss about it. That was what Emily had done. Either that or running away, and she wasn't going to do that either. Instead, she reached for her anger, because that at least made her feel strong.

'And if I did?' she asked shortly. 'What would you do at night without me in your bed?'

A muscle ticced in the side of his jaw, a sure sign of his own temper rising. 'I would survive.'

So, after the intense passion they'd shared and then insisting on a full marriage, he was now completely happy for her to move out?

The hurt inside her deepened, a knife twisting in her gut. It was so much a reminder of her marriage to Edward that it was painful. Edward might have chosen her, but he hadn't fought for their relationship, and he hadn't fought for her. When he'd been unhappy, he'd turned around and gone after her sister instead.

'Okay, so you're absolutely fine with me living somewhere else, then.' She knew she was starting to sound shrill and yet she couldn't help herself. 'And you don't apparently care whether I'm around or not. I get it. But I did think the whole point of this marriage was to create a family for Diego.'

The muscle in his jaw leapt again. 'It is. I'm not the one threatening to live somewhere else.'

Her anger twisted hard. Did he really not understand? Perhaps he didn't. Yet that would mean having to tell him that she was lonely. That she wanted more than this. More from him. How could she though, when she didn't even know what more she wanted?

Then again, if she didn't tell him, how would he know?

'It's isolating, Sebastián,' she said, trying not to sound as pathetic as she feared she might. 'And it's lonely. I uprooted my whole life to come here and yet for the past two weeks I've been alone with nothing but Diego for company. Which is fine, but he's a baby. He can't exactly have a conversation with me.'

Something shifted in Sebastián's eyes, a flicker of what looked like surprise, but it was gone before she could read it. 'What do you want, then?' he asked. 'I'm busy during the day and you get plenty of attention at night.'

'I'm not talking about sex,' she snapped. 'Some adult conversation might be nice.'

'Fine. What do you want to talk about?'

He didn't want to talk to her. He really couldn't be clearer.

The needle of hurt dug deeper. Again, this felt like what had happened with her and Edward, her constantly pushing and him retreating, giving her what she wanted and yet always in ways that felt placating. It had always felt false. She hated it.

Suddenly her appetite for argument vanished, leaving her with a bone-deep emotional exhaustion that had nothing to do with lack of sleep and more to do with spending two weeks fighting grief and an intense desire for a man who apparently wanted nothing from her but sex.

'Forget it,' she said, abruptly turning away. 'I've changed my mind.'

The air felt tight around him, as if her entering the stables had somehow tipped the oxygen right out of it. She had on one of the loose summer dresses she'd taken to wearing around the hacienda, this one in a deep golden yellow, and it made her skin look gilded, her eyes like the darkest espresso, and her hair as if there were threads of gold running through the glossy black strands.

She was so beautiful. She was also hurt and angry, and all thanks to him.

He should let her walk away, let her take that hurt and anger with her, but while he could stand her temper, he couldn't bear to hurt her. Emily had told him the same thing about life at the hacienda being lonely and isolating, yet it hadn't been time with him that Emily had wanted. She'd wanted to go back to the city, to shop and eat at fancy restaurants, and go out to nightclubs and parties. Oh, she'd wanted him to come with her and he'd gone a couple of times, but those things weren't to his taste. He preferred the quiet of the countryside, spending time with the horses, going riding and hiking in the mountains, or simply sitting in the hacienda courtyard with a good book.

Alice wasn't asking for any of the things Emily had. All she'd wanted was some conversation. It wasn't much, and yet she couldn't have asked for anything more dangerous. Mainly because he'd been trying to set boundaries around their marriage for the past two weeks.

He'd realised not long after they'd returned from Madrid that he was on a precipice. That the more time he spent with Alice, the closer to the edge he got and if he wasn't careful, he was going to let his desire for her carry him straight over it.

The fantasies he'd had of being able to have her whenever he wanted and no one to stop them this time had been heady and intense, and also too much. So he'd decided that keeping himself distant during the day and only letting the leash off at night, in bed, was the answer. Made sure it all stayed about sex and nothing else.

There had to be clear boundaries. His emotions always led him astray and then he'd end up failing the people who mattered to him, the way he'd done with Mateo and Emily, and he wasn't doing that again. He couldn't. He didn't want to give Alice any false expectations either.

So yes, he should let her walk away and yet he found himself reaching for her all the same, his fingers closing around her bare arm and holding on tight, stopping her from leaving. 'Wait,' he said in a low voice.

She halted and turned back to him, and, even

though she was trying to hide it, he could see the hurt glinting in her dark eyes.

Dios. He'd been a bastard to her.

'I'm sorry,' he said, hating her hurt and wanting to give her the truth, because she deserved it. 'I know what you gave up to come here and marry me, that it was a sacrifice. You did it for Diego and I appreciate that. He is the most important thing in the world to me, and knowing you will be a mother to him is the best outcome I could have hoped for.'

She stared up at him, her lush mouth losing the hardness around it, the glint of hurt in her eyes easing. Her skin was so warm beneath his fingertips, and he could feel his desire for her begin to coil like thick smoke in his veins.

'But I've been deliberately putting distance between us these past two weeks, Alice,' he went on. 'And yes, it's because of you.'

Surprise flickered over her face. 'Why?' Then the surprise faded, leaving yet more hurt behind it. 'What did I do?'

Look at you. You failed Emily and now you're failing Alice.

No, he wouldn't. He couldn't hurt her the way he'd hurt Emily. He tugged her closer. 'You did nothing,' he said. 'The problem is me.'

She gave him a searching look. 'How?'

It was going to be difficult to articulate the complicated need he had for her. The strange compulsion that had gripped him the moment he'd first seen her, that had caused him to constantly crave her presence even though he was married to her sister.

He knew it wasn't love. He'd already experienced love and it was cruel. Love had made his mother betray her vows and caused his father's bitter resentment. Love had made him a target for Mateo's anger and been the reason Javier had lost his job. Love wasn't something he'd ever wanted to give anyone else, though he'd tried to give Emily a facsimile of it and it had caused her nothing but heartache.

He couldn't make that same mistake with Alice.

'When you're around I...can't think,' he said slowly. 'I can't do anything but imagine you beneath me and it's...consuming. It interferes with everything. I told you, it's an obsession, and there has to be some boundaries, understand? It's easier to keep my distance.'

'Easier for you, you mean?'

He could deny it, give her some lie and then walk away, but he couldn't do that. It wouldn't be fair, not to either of them. 'Yes,' he said bluntly.

'So what about me? Am I supposed to...what? Just accept that I can't even talk to you? Is that what you're saying?'

'Alice—'

'How is that fair? I'm not asking for your heart on a plate, Sebastián. Only a conversation.'

His fingers tightened on her arm, frustration coiling through him. 'It will never be just a conversation, that's what I'm trying to tell you.'

'So? What are you so afraid of?'

'You,' he said before he could stop himself. 'I'm afraid of falling for you.'

The words crashed into the silence like stones through a window, shattering the nice little lie he'd told himself that this was all about physical obsession.

He didn't want to fall for her. His first wife was only two months dead and he'd failed her.

Just as you failed your father. Just as you failed Javier.

And that was the truth, wasn't it? He hadn't been his father's son and he hadn't been Javier's, even though he was Mateo's by adoption and Javier's by blood. He'd been nobody's. And so nothing he'd done had ever been good enough.

It won't be good enough for her either...

Alice pulled her arm from his grasp and took a small step back, her eyes still wide and dark. The flickering emotions in them made his breath catch.

She shook her head. 'That's...not... I can't...'

'Of course not,' he said, so she didn't have to explain. 'It's too soon after Emily's death and now I have Diego.'

She glanced away, lifting a hand to her mouth, her fingers trembling. 'You said it was nothing more than sex.' Her voice was slightly hoarse. 'That's what you said in Madrid.'

He'd shocked her, he could see that. And it was clear that love wasn't something she wanted either. A part of him was satisfied by that and yet another part found it...

No. He couldn't think about that. It would lead him one step closer to the precipice and he wasn't going to do that. 'Yes,' he said reluctantly, 'I did.'

Her dark eyes came to his again. 'So maybe…we need to find out once and for all. Maybe if we have no limits, no boundaries, we can…keep doing whatever we want until this…obsession is all gone.'

The idea had merit. In Madrid, she'd said that perhaps part of the appeal had been how forbidden each of them had been to the other, and even though he'd denied it at the time, maybe she hadn't been wrong. In which case putting limits on his hunger would of course make her even more appealing to him.

So…perhaps if he took the limits off completely, indulged in every single one of his fantasies whenever and wherever he liked, not just at night but during the day too, that would make his own hunger less intense. It was worth considering.

Maybe if he spent time with her, if they lost themselves totally in each other, they'd discover that what this instant chemistry between them had been all along was only physical attraction and the allure of the forbidden. An illusion giving the impression of a depth that wasn't there.

'Are you sure that's a good idea?' he asked.

Slowly Alice lifted her chin. 'I don't want to fall for you any more than you want to fall for me, because you're right. It's too soon. I lost my sister and Edward, and Diego is more important than anything. How can we give him the family he needs when we're so consumed by what we feel for each other anyway? We need to know. We need to find out. Or at least get rid of the…want. Neither of us want love, Sebastián, so perhaps it will work out.'

She was right, especially about Diego. This constant uncertainty when it came to her and what he felt wouldn't be a good foundation on which to build the kind of family he wanted for his son. They needed to burn out their need for each other and do it without distractions, so they could then decide what their marriage would be like going forward. And with Diego front and centre.

His heartbeat was suddenly loud, desire rising inside him, relentless and all-consuming. Her, with no boundaries, no limits… They hadn't had a honeymoon—he hadn't thought they'd need one, but perhaps that had been a mistake. Perhaps a honeymoon was exactly what they should have, and away from the hacienda. Away from the memories of Emily and Edward and the Christmases they'd spent here. Away from the ghosts of his own marriage and his failure.

A honeymoon where there were no memories. Where they could find out what *their* marriage looked like in a place that was theirs and only theirs.

'If you could go anywhere in the world,' he asked abruptly, 'where would you go?'

Alice blinked. 'What? What's that got to do with anything?'

'We didn't have a honeymoon and I think that was a mistake.'

She gave him a wary look. 'So, you're saying we should have one?'

'Yes. Away from the hacienda and the memories here. Away from everything. If we know what we don't want, then we can decide what we do.'

She nodded slowly. 'Okay. But we do it together. You don't make decisions like putting distance between us for me and I don't make them for you.'

That was fair. He should have said something to her about that, he should have been clearer.

Already you're failing.

No, no, he wouldn't, not this time. Not with her.

'So,' he said, allowing the need that was strangling him to deepen his voice. 'In the interests of making decisions together, tell me where you want to go.'

Something lit slowly in her eyes and he felt warmth settle just behind his breastbone in response. It had been a long time since he'd put that light in anyone's eyes, in fact the last time had been when he'd bought Emily her Paris apartment. Then there had been a bitterness in him at the gift, because what he'd actually been giving her was his absence, and that was what had made her look so pleased. Not with Alice though. A honeymoon meant time spent in each other's presence and it was clear that was exactly what she wanted.

She wanted to spend time with him.

Her mouth curved and the warmth deepened. This was the first time he'd made her smile. 'Okay, well, I like sun and I like swimming. Nice food obviously. I also love beaches and being on the ocean.'

Good. He liked all of those things too. 'No sight-seeing?'

'I don't know if that's the point of this, is it?'

No, it wasn't. The point was seeing each other, not other things.

'Fine. Will you leave the decision to me?'

She tilted her head slightly, her mouth curving even more. 'I like how you're not really giving me the option.'

There was a teasing note in her voice, only slight, but it was there, and it made the warmth spread through him, thawing parts of him that had been frozen for a long time. Perhaps even since his father had made it very clear just how wide the gap between them was and how it was up to him to bridge it. He wasn't actually Mateo's son after all, so *he* had to be the one to do the work.

And suddenly he couldn't stand the distance between them. If there were no limits and no boundaries, if they were going to test what this thing actually was between them, then he didn't have to fight any of his urges. In fact, it was better if he actively indulged them.

So he crossed the space separating them and pulled her into his arms. 'Do you want the option?'

'No,' she said without hesitation, her palms coming to rest on his chest. 'In fact, you can arrange everything if you like.'

The warmth was changing now, becoming the kind of heat it always did whenever he was touching her, whenever he was even near her. A fire, a blaze, all-consuming, devastating.

'Good,' he said. 'And this honeymoon? It starts now.'

Then he bent his head and took her mouth like a man starving.

CHAPTER NINE

ALICE LAY ON the blanket on the sand and watched Sebastián stride from the sea, magnificently naked, drops of water and brilliant sunshine delineating every hard-cut muscle of his powerful body. His tan had deepened, providing a rich foil to the smoky gold of his eyes, the colour standing out even more as he came towards her across the sand.

Her stomach clenched. Everything clenched. He was so beautiful and he was her husband. Hers.

Your husband who doesn't love you.

That was true, but they'd already decided back in Spain that love wouldn't feature in their marriage. There were too many reasons why it wasn't a good idea. They'd both lost their spouses and her heart was still broken and bleeding, and she couldn't risk giving it to someone else. Especially someone who didn't want it anyway.

What about later? When the grief has eased? What about then?

Alice pushed the thought out of her mind. There was no point thinking about the future and she didn't want to anyway. Not when the present was so much better. The present with *him* filling every moment of it.

She could hardly believe how much she wanted him. In fact she seemed to have an endless capacity. A hunger that didn't seem to be getting any better no matter how many times they indulged it, and they'd indulged it *a lot* since they'd arrived.

Sebastián had kept their final destination a surprise and it wasn't until they were in a smaller plane from Belize City and flying over the Belize Barrier Reef in the Caribbean that Sebastián had told her where they were going.

A villa on a tiny, private and very remote island. There were no other people on the island, and, apart from a small cottage on a neighbouring island that housed the staff who managed the villa, there was no one else within miles.

The island had the most beautiful white sand beaches surrounding it and the villa itself was sprawling and open-plan, with massive floor-to-ceiling windows that doubled as doors so one entire wall could be opened up. There were lazy fans and dark wooden floors and the master bedroom had a huge four-poster bed hung with gauzy white curtains.

It was the most utterly perfect place she could imagine.

The first couple of days were spent entirely sating themselves physically with each other, neither of them holding back. They didn't talk, but talking hadn't been the point, at least not initially. That could wait until their physical hunger was at least at a reasonable level.

After the intensity had eased a little, they explored the island, spending hours in the water and lying on the beach. There was a small boat for their use and Sebastián piloted it out to the nearby reef where they snorkelled amongst multicoloured coral and fish. It was astonishingly beautiful.

He refused to let her do a thing, cooking for her and bringing her treats, making sure her every wish was catered to, and she loved it. Her and Edward's honeymoon had been spent in Italy and, while she'd enjoyed it, even then she'd had the nagging feeling that Edward had been far more interested in sightseeing than in spending time with her.

She had no such doubts about Sebastián. She was what interested him, and he made no secret of it. She'd never felt so desired. Except his interest seemed to be limited to the here and now, what they were doing that day and what she'd like for dinner and whether she'd like having her hands tied to the headboard of the bed as he made love to her.

Perhaps he was waiting to talk more until later, or perhaps he was waiting for her to broach the topic first. Either way though, it made a subtle tension run through her, a nameless doubt she couldn't shake.

He came up now to the blanket she was lying on, beneath a pavilion hung with shade cloth to protect them both from the sun, water dripping from his magnificent body as he picked up a towel and dried himself off.

She made a cursory protest as water scattered over her bare skin, but she didn't really mind, not when she was enjoying watching the play of water on his tanned skin. He dropped the towel and lay down on his side beside her, his head propped on his hand. When he smiled, her heart turned over in her chest.

'I'm afraid of falling for you,' he'd said back in Spain.

She hadn't been able to get it out of her head. He'd been honest, his gaze fierce, yet there had been a grim note in his voice when he'd said it.

A shiver at the memory went through her. She'd been shocked. Firstly that he'd been anywhere close to falling for her, which she hadn't known, and secondly, that her initial reaction had been one of pure, unadulterated joy.

In fact, if she thought about it now, she could still feel the warmth of that joy, like the Caribbean sun blazing in her heart. She'd struggled to cover it because there had been no joy in his face, no joy in his voice either. He'd said it as if falling for her would be the worst thing in the world.

That had hurt, made the knife twist hard inside her, but she was good at masking her emotions, so she'd made sure that hurt didn't show. It was fine if he didn't want to love her. Love had always been a fraught emotion, full of high expectations and crushing disappointments, of giving and giving and getting nothing in return. Of feeling as if she wasn't good enough for anyone. Not for her parents, not for Edward. And maybe in the end, not enough for Emily either. Because if she had been, would Emily have had an affair with Alice's husband?

Really, she was better off without it, and most especially from him.

Yet no matter what she told herself, she could still feel that joy inside her. The bright spark of possibility that refused to be ignored. And looking into his eyes now, she couldn't help the rogue thought that whispered just how good it would be to be loved by him. To have all his fierce passion directed on her, and not just the physical passion. The emotional intensity that had had him claim Diego and refuse to give him up.

You want that. You want to be claimed. You want to be loved and loved passionately. You're hungry for it.

Her throat closed with longing. Well, who wouldn't be hungry for it? But it didn't have to be with him. She could find some other man like him who didn't have all the baggage and who was ready to love and be loved in return.

But there are no other men like him and you know that.

She tore her gaze away from his mesmerising smile. It wasn't true. There were plenty of men like him. Men with smoky golden eyes and fierce passion and intensity. Men who blazed with desire when she touched them. Men who wanted her just as fiercely as she wanted them…

The strange grief in her throat got worse. No, she was lying to herself. It was true. There were no other men like him. He was the only one. And she could tell herself all she liked that she'd find someone else and fall in love with him, but the truth was that wasn't going to happen.

No. Because you're in love with him and you have been ever since the day you met him.

Cold prickled all over her skin, her stomach dropping, and she had to stare hard at the brilliant turquoise of the lagoon to control her expression. Her heart was thundering in her chest so loud she could barely hear anything else.

Love at first sight. The lightning bolt from the blue. She'd never believed in it. She hadn't loved Edward at first sight. That had grown over the years he and she and Emily were at school. Maybe that was why she hadn't recognised what she'd felt for Sebastián when it had happened. Because she hadn't believed it would ever happen to her and yet… It had. She was in love with him, completely and utterly and she had been for the past five years. But she'd been married so she'd minimised it, told herself it was just some strange attraction she didn't understand. Yet it had never been that.

He doesn't want to love you in return.

She tried to ignore the lump of pain and grief that choked her. She couldn't let that matter. She had to pretend that all of this was just sexual attraction and nothing more, because maybe if she did, it would go away. She certainly couldn't tell him how she felt, not when doing so might ruin this special time together. And especially not when he'd been perfectly clear about what he wanted and what he didn't.

'Alice?' he asked, his voice full of concern. 'What's wrong?'

Forcing away her emotions, she swallowed hard and braced herself before glancing back at him. Somehow she managed to produce a smile. 'Nothing. Only... sometimes you're just too gorgeous to even look at.'

He laughed, which made everything worse, because the sound was so warm and so devastatingly attractive. She could listen to him laugh until the end of time. 'I know the feeling,' he said, his gaze turning molten as it ran over her in blatant appreciation. 'Though I think I can force myself.'

Inevitable arousal moved like a tide through her veins. God, how she loved the way he looked at her. She was as naked as he was and the obvious delight he took in her nakedness had gone a long way to boosting her confidence in her body. She'd even come to enjoy wearing nothing, especially since it meant he wore nothing too.

Yet another reason to love him.

She fought to keep the smile on her face, to not let any trace of her thoughts show. Luckily his attention had dropped to her stomach. He frowned slightly then reached to trace her surgery scar. She'd been very aware of it initially, the first time she'd been naked with him, but he hadn't made any comment about it or drawn attention to it, and gradually she'd lost her self-consciousness.

Now though, as his fingers brushed over the thin white line just above her pubic bone, she tensed.

He glanced up immediately. 'You don't want me touching you here?'

She swallowed again, trying to relax. 'No, it's fine.'

'It's not fine. You're tense.'

'It doesn't hurt, if that's what you're asking. It's just…'

'Painful in other ways,' he finished for her.

What could she say other than the truth? 'Yes,' she said simply. 'It is.'

He kept his hand where it was, his fingertips tracing the line of her scar with such gentleness that the full, aching feeling already in her heart became heavy and raw. 'I'm so sorry this happened to you,' he murmured. 'You wanted children quite badly, didn't you?'

She didn't know why he was choosing now to talk about this, and, given how emotionally fragile she felt already, she should have found both his question and his touch intrusive. Yet she didn't. He was so gentle and maybe that was why her heart hurt so much. Because she could hear the sympathy in his voice, as if what had happened to her was important to him, as if it mattered.

Yet another reason to love him.

For some inexplicable reasons tears prickled in her eyes, though she fought them back. 'I did,' she said huskily. 'And it wasn't just the baby and its future I lost, but also any possibility of having another and all the futures that went with it.'

His gaze was warm, his fingers still tracing her scar gently, as if he were soothing it and her. 'When did it happen?'

'About two years after Edward and I got married. It was my…first pregnancy.'

He glanced down at the scar. 'I saw a light go out inside you at some point. I always wondered what happened. Now I know you were grieving.'

A little shock ran through her that he'd noticed the change in her because no one else had apart from Emily. But yes, he was right, she'd been grieving.

'Edward wanted to move on,' she said, even though it felt disloyal to say. 'He was kind, don't get me wrong, but he thought the sooner we put it behind us, the better. He didn't want to discuss it either. He mentioned surrogates and adoptions initially, but…' She stopped, stripped bare by the pain of the memories even though it had been years ago, and by another, somehow deeper pain that had only just occurred to her. Sebastián wanted more children yet she would never be able to give them to him. She would never carry his baby. Never.

The knife in her heart twisted.

'Alice,' Sebastián said, his expression full of concern. 'We don't have to talk about it if it's too painful.'

She set her jaw, forcing away the hurt the way she always did. 'No, it's okay. It's been years and I'm over it.'

He said nothing for a long moment, looking at her, the compassion in his eyes making her want to weep despite everything. 'Were you ever allowed to grieve properly?' he asked softly. 'Were you ever allowed to mourn?'

The question felt as if he were twisting in the knife even harder, yet there was nothing but understanding in his expression. Grief was no stranger to either of them, she realised, and he knew loss when he saw it.

'No,' she admitted. 'I don't think I was. I don't think I…let myself grieve. Edward was patient with me but…' She swallowed, wanting to say it even though, again, it was another disloyal thought. 'I always had the impression that he wasn't as upset about it as I was and that he didn't think it was as important as I did. Even later, he never followed up on adoptions or anything.' She took a breath, suddenly weighed down by grief. 'I'll never be able to have your child, Sebastián. Never.' She hadn't meant to cry and yet there were tears in her eyes, and then his hands were reaching for her, pulling her close, his arms folding around her.

He didn't speak, only held her, and somehow the warmth of his presence and the strength of his arms had her weeping into his chest as the pain cut its way through her heart. He remained silent, holding her tightly, giving her space to grieve for the baby she lost and all those futures. For her failure of a marriage and for the husband who hadn't really loved her. And for her sister, whom she'd loved even though she'd betrayed her.

Eventually her sobs ran dry and he kept holding her, stroking her hair and murmuring soft words in Spanish that were inexplicably comforting.

Another reason to love him.

Her eyes were scratchy and her throat was sore and her heart ached and ached. She wished passionately that the day she'd met him she'd been true to her heart and recognised the feeling for what it was. That she'd been honest with her husband and left him instead of fighting for something that neither of them had wanted any more.

But she hadn't. And now all she was left with was her broken, shattered heart that somehow still managed to beat for a man who thought the worst thing in the world would be to love her back.

She had no idea what she was going to do.

'I could tell you that I don't care that you won't have my child,' Sebastián said after a long moment, his deep voice rumbling in her ear. 'I do care. But I also care about you and your pain. But you know that Diego will be our child in every way there is. And we will have more, I promise it.'

It *did* matter to him. It did. That was what she'd wanted from Edward, just some sign that he felt the loss too, yet Edward had never given it to her. But Sebastián had. And it felt good to know he felt the same way, and also that he felt all wasn't lost.

Of course they would have Diego and others, too.

She lifted her damp face from his chest, and looked up at his hard, carved features. His expression was fierce, as was the burning look in his eyes. It was clear that this was a promise he intended to keep.

Yet another reason to love him.

She wished she didn't keep thinking that. She wished her heart would stop reminding her that this man was the only one for her.

'What about Emily?' she asked, her voice still thick with tears. 'Did you want children with her?'

He reached to gently brush the tears from her face. 'Yes. But she didn't, not right away. She wanted to wait a few years. That was okay with me initially, because I was busy in the stables. I didn't insist either, because I wanted to give her time to adjust to our marriage and to living in Spain.' He pushed a curl behind her ear. 'Like Edward, she didn't want to have the discussion about children. She kept avoiding it. And then Diego arrived.'

'You really thought he was yours?'

'I had no reason to believe otherwise. And when I did find out, it genuinely made no difference to how I felt about him. In fact, after I found out I became even more certain that he would be my son.'

'Why? Because of your father?'

'Yes. I couldn't let any child grow up the way I did. Mateo was resentful of me for not truly being his. I was the evidence of my mother's faithlessness and that needled him but, since I was also the only way he'd ever get an heir, there wasn't much else he could do.'

The aching grief in her chest had gradually sub-sided and all she wanted was to lie here in his arms and ask him questions about his childhood. She was hungry for information now.

'Did he hurt you?' she asked, concerned.

'No.' Sebastián gently stroked the crease between her brows. 'Don't worry, *mi cielo*, he didn't. Not physi-cally. He was…exacting. Demanding. A jealous man too. I used to love visiting the stables, because I loved the horses, and I spent a lot of time with Javier, who was the best stable manager we ever had. Javier didn't know I was his and I didn't know he was my biologi-cal father, not then. I just knew I liked being with him. Mateo became very jealous of the time I spent with him and eventually he fired Javier and told me that Javier had lost his job because of me. Because I was disloyal and ungrateful.'

Her heart seized at the blunt words. 'That sounds… awful.'

His eyes glinted as he looked at her. 'Mateo already had an unfaithful wife, and he drew the line at hav-ing an unfaithful son. Especially when that son was actually the son of his wife's lover.'

'Still,' she said. 'That doesn't excuse him being awful to you. It wasn't fair of him to treat you like that. It wasn't your fault that you weren't his. It's not as if you were allowed to choose your own father.'

'No,' he agreed. 'But then being Javier's son wasn't the only reason he resented me.'

'There was another reason?'

'Yes.' The glitter in his eyes became sharper, harder. 'He told me that I'd killed my mother.'

Alice's eyes went wide with shock and concern. He'd been too blunt but that was exactly what Mateo had told him and in just that way. Making him feel like a murderer.

He shouldn't have said anything about it, of course, but she'd asked and there was no reason not to tell her. She should know about his bitter childhood so she'd understand what he hoped to avoid with Diego.

She was beautiful here, lying naked against his chest with the warm Caribbean salt-scented air feathering over both of them. Her hair was a wild tangle over her shoulders, and she still had the flower behind her ear that he'd put there that morning, a hibiscus blooming pink and gold and red.

Her eyes were red from her moment of grief for her lost baby and her lost fertility, the tracks of her tears still shiny on her skin. The sight of them made him ache.

He shouldn't have made their first discussion about that loss, not when it was obviously still so painful for her, but when he'd come out of the water and dropped down beside her, that scar on her belly was all he could see. He knew what it was and he hadn't wanted to say anything about it earlier, and yet after spending days making love to her, knowing it was there and knowing what it meant… He couldn't keep ignoring it.

Her lost child, her lost fertility, her lost marriage

were all things they needed to talk about, just as they needed to talk about their future and their own marriage. Everything had remained so unspoken between them for so long and they couldn't keep doing that.

So he'd touched that scar gently, tracing the line of it over her warm skin.

She hadn't held back when he'd asked her about it and when she'd starkly said that she'd never have his child, and he'd seen the grief in her eyes, he'd felt the same grief inside himself too. Both at realising that, yes, he wanted her to carry his child, and yet knowing she never would.

That it felt painful to him meant that the edge of the precipice was even nearer than he'd thought, and that he'd have to be careful. Yet he'd pulled her into his arms to comfort her instead, unable to stop himself.

Years ago he'd wanted to do the same thing when he'd seen the light inside her go out, but back then it hadn't been his place to do so.

He was her husband now, though, and it was definitely his place, and, regardless of whether it was a good idea or not, he was going to give her comfort and space to grieve however he could.

They had to be able to talk to each other in order to build a healthy relationship between them. A relationship that would provide the best environment for Diego to grow up in.

Now, Alice was looking up at him, her eyes dark. 'What do you mean you killed her?'

He tried never to think about that day in his father's office. It had been a long time ago, yet, despite the years, it still felt as if his father with those words had reached inside his chest and gouged out his heart. The simple cruelty of it, to an eleven-year-old boy, still bothered him.

Another reason why you can't fall in love with her.

Of course not. He'd seen the true face of love that day and it was petty and cruel and jealous. He wanted no part of it ever again.

'Mateo never told me how my mother died,' he said. 'And no one knew that I wasn't Mateo's son. And until the day he fired Javier, not even I knew.'

Alice look aghast. 'What? You mean he kept that all from you, only to dump it all on you then? Why?'

His father's face had been red with fury and Sebastián had been bewildered as to why. He'd thought that his spending time with the horses was what Mateo wanted, especially learning from Javier, the most experienced of the stable hands.

'Mateo was jealous,' he said. 'And vindictive. And he was furious that I'd spent more time with my biological father than him. He accused me of being as faithless and ungrateful as my mother. Then he told me that she'd had an affair with Javier, that I was Javier's son and that my mother had died having me. And he told me all of that for no other reason than to hurt me.'

'Oh, Sebastián,' Alice breathed, her expression full of deep sympathy and a flickering hurt that he knew was for him. 'I'm so sorry.'

He wasn't sure why the rest of the words spilled out, given what they revealed, but they did. 'He told me I was a poor replacement for her, that I wasn't who he would have chosen for a son. But I was all he'd had to work with and so I'd have to do.'

Her hands had pressed flat against his chest, the look in her dark eyes making him ache. 'What a terrible thing to say to a child. And how cruel.'

Yes. Mateo *had* been cruel and vindictive, and needlessly petty. But Sebastián knew why. He'd loved his wife and she'd been unfaithful to him and had a child by another man. Sebastián's mere presence hit Mateo in a place where he was most sensitive—his male pride.

Another reason why you can't love her, no matter how understanding she is. No matter how much you want to.

It was true. He didn't know if his mother had loved Javier, but they'd clearly formed enough of a bond that she'd been unfaithful to her husband for him. And he had been the result. Just as he was the cause of his mother's death.

After his father had told him the bitter truth, he hadn't known what to do. All he'd known was that he was the cause of so much unhappiness and so the only way forward seemed to be trying his hardest to make up for it.

Except Mateo had made it very clear that nothing Sebastián did ever would.

It still doesn't.

'I got over it,' he said, pushing the thought away. 'Though my father made it very obvious that nothing I could do would make up for her loss. He wasn't very good at hiding his resentment or his jealousy, and I think if I hadn't had the horses I might have eventually decided it wasn't worth it and left. But they were what kept me there.'

Her fingertips were warm on his skin, her gaze dark and deep, piercing him right through. She'd always seemed to see more than he wanted her to. More than Emily had. He hadn't told Emily about his father, for example, mainly because Emily had never asked.

'That's why you care about the horses,' Alice murmured. 'Why you love them. They accepted you.'

How she somehow knew that, he wasn't sure, but it was true nonetheless.

He stroked his thumb across her cheekbone, relishing the feel of her skin. 'They did. They were much more accepting than my father ever was. All a horse needs is some good hay, clean water and kindness, and maybe an apple now and then. They don't require anything else and they don't need you to be anything else.'

'I understand,' she said. 'No wonder you spent a lot of time with them.' She paused a moment, her dark brows drawing together. 'You know that your father was wrong, don't you? And that the horses were right. He should have learned from them. He should have accepted you the way you were, just like you accepted Diego.'

A thread of impatience wound through him. He

didn't want to keep talking about this, because what was the point? The past was immutable. He couldn't change it now even if he wanted to.

'Perhaps,' he said, dismissive. 'But he didn't. And in his mind, my mother's death was my fault and so how could anything I do ever make up for that?' He'd been bitter once, but he'd lost that over the years, because there was no reason to dwell on it. Mateo hadn't accepted him and had continued to blame him right up to the day he died, and it was what it was.

Alice reached up and took his face between her hands, her fingertips cool on his cheeks. 'You're not supposed to make up for it,' she said. 'You were a child. A baby. You didn't do anything to anyone.'

'I know that,' he said. 'But he blamed me for it anyway.'

'He shouldn't have,' Alice said insistently. 'He might have been grieving and angry, and all of those things, but that was *his* issue. He shouldn't have made it yours.'

But there must have been something bad about you, something wrong. Why else would he have been so cruel? Why else would you have caused such unhappiness to so many people?

Something twisted painfully in his heart, as if she'd touched on an old wound, an old doubt that had festered even though he'd tried to forget it.

'Perhaps I should have helped him,' he said, even though he didn't want to say it. 'Perhaps there was something I could have done to make it better.'

Alice's fingers pressed a little harder. 'Tell me,' she said, that light in her eyes that had drawn him to her so powerfully flickering. 'If Emily had died having Diego, would you have told him the same thing eventually? That he killed her? Would you expect him as a little boy to make it up to you?'

A shock went through him, bringing with it a ferocious protectiveness. 'No,' he said flatly before he'd even thought it through. 'Never.'

'No,' she echoed. 'And there was no excuse for him to treat you like that, either. You didn't deserve it, Sebastián.'

There was so much conviction in her voice, so much warmth in her eyes that he teetered on the edge of the precipice, the wind threatening to take him over. It would be so easy to fall, so very easy. To name what he felt for her as love and let it take him.

But he couldn't. He already had one person in his life that had a claim on his heart—Diego. The thought of potentially failing him was crushing enough. He didn't want to add any more weight to the one he was already carrying.

'Whether I deserved it or not doesn't matter,' he said. 'But now you know why I will put Diego and his happiness before everything else. Why I want him to have a mother as well as a father. Why I want him to have a family, somewhere safe where he feels he belongs.'

Her gaze flickered, as if something about his response had disappointed her, though he wasn't sure what it had been.

This is how it starts. Failing her.

No, he wouldn't. This time it would be different, he'd make sure of it. Love wasn't a possibility but he'd give her everything else. A home. Children. Comfort. Companionship. He'd support her career too and anything she chose to do. She could have just about everything she wanted.

They could have it.

And if she wants more?

But she didn't want more. She'd told him back in Spain that she didn't want love, that she felt the same way he did about it, and besides, she'd agreed to marry him. He'd told her what to expect and she'd still said yes.

Doesn't she deserve love, though? After everything she's lost?

Oh, she did. She deserved to be loved completely and utterly, but he wasn't going to be the one to give it to her. And if that meant she'd eventually leave him and find someone else who would, then he'd have to deal with that. He would never get in the way of her finding happiness, even if that was with another man.

Even if that thought makes you feral with rage.

He ignored the thought, shoved it away. That was a thought his father would have, one of those jealous, vindictive thoughts and he wouldn't be like him. Ever. If Alice wanted to leave him, he'd let her go, but… That didn't mean he couldn't make the decision a difficult one. In fact, he'd make it as hard for her to leave him as he could.

He turned her in his lap so she was facing him, her thighs spread on either side of his hips, the soft, damp heat of her sex pressing against his aching shaft. She gave one of those delicious little shivers that she always did whenever she was aroused, the darkness of her eyes seeming to glow and get molten.

'Of course you do,' she murmured. 'I want all those things for him too.'

'I know you do.' He settled one hand on her hip while he slid the other between her thighs, stroking the hot, soft folds he found there, making her gasp. 'But that doesn't mean that there can't be anything for us.'

She moaned, her hips flexing, arching against his hand. She was already wet for him, her nipples hard, her skin flushed. 'Such as?' she asked, her voice husky.

'This.' He moved his hand and gripped her other hip, sliding into her in one long, slow, deep thrust. 'And it's not just sex, *mi cielo*…my sky.' His voice had roughened at the tight clasp of her sex around his. 'It *is* more. We have a connection and it's not only physical.'

She slid her arms around his neck, her lovely body pressing hard against his. Her eyes had gone very dark, inches from his own, and he was captivated by the currents in them, light and shadow like the sun moving over a dark river.

'What else is it, then?' she asked softly. 'Tell me.'

He couldn't look away from the emotion shifting in

her gaze. He began to move, watching as the building pleasure became part of those currents, turning into something powerful and deep, glowing in her eyes. 'It is emotional too,' he said, his voice even rougher. 'And I will be there for you, understand me? I will give you everything you need to be happy. Because your happiness is as important to me as Diego's.'

She stared back at him, unflinching, those currents in her eyes shifting and swirling. But she didn't speak, she only leaned forward and kissed him, her mouth hot and open and sweet. Yet he could also taste desperation, though he wasn't sure what she was so desperate about.

Are you certain? Are you certain you don't know?

But he pushed that thought aside as the pleasure began to get deeper, wider, and soon he wasn't thinking at all. There was only the rhythm between them and the friction that drove him out of his mind, the heat and the blazing passion that always seared both of them down to their souls.

And if a small, nagging doubt crept into his heart, it was soon lost under the relentless tide of ecstasy, as it washed over both of them and carried them away.

CHAPTER TEN

ALICE WALKED SLOWLY over pristine white sand still warm from the heat of the day, her hand held securely in Sebastián's as he walked beside her. They'd taken to having evening strolls along the beach to watch the sunset, sometimes talking idly about their day, sometimes not speaking at all and just enjoying each other's company.

It was peaceful and usually she relished this time with him. But tonight was their last night on the island. Tomorrow they'd be returning to Spain, and she couldn't shake the tension that coiled inside her.

All this would be ending and she didn't want to think about how it would be between them once they returned to the hacienda. Back to her life as Sebastián's wife in every way, except one.

Abruptly, he came to a stop and let go of her hand, bending to pick something up off the sand. 'For you, *mi cielo*,' he murmured and held it out to her.

It was a shell, polished by the sea and the sand, gleaming in the light of the setting sun, its smooth white surface stained pink and gold and red.

'Oh,' she breathed, taking it from him and turning it over in her palm to examine it. 'It's beautiful.'

He smiled, genuine and warm, his eyes full of the familiar heat that always stole her breath clean away. 'Yes,' he said, 'it is.'

But he wasn't looking at the shell. He was looking at her.

Her heart ached in her chest and her throat closed. She'd never get enough of the compliments he gave her, never. And when he gave them, she always felt as beautiful as he told her she was. For the first time in years.

Will he say those things to you back in Spain, too? Will he still look at you the way he's doing now? Or will that heat in his eyes grow colder? Will he stop looking at you at all...?

Alice tore her gaze from his, directing it out over the ocean instead, the agonising pressure of all that love in her heart like a weight, crushing her.

It had become even worse after that day on the beach when he'd told her about his father and the terrible things he'd said to Sebastián. How he'd made a lonely little boy feel as if he'd failed. She'd hurt for him so much. She knew what it was like to believe that you weren't enough, to feel as if you'd disappointed people.

It wasn't fair and it wasn't right, and she'd wanted more than anything to help him understand that he hadn't deserved it and that nothing he did was a failure. That he couldn't blame himself for his mother's death or his father's inability to accept him.

He hadn't brought up the subject again, so perhaps she hadn't succeeded.

'If I didn't know any better,' she said with forced lightness, shoving the drag of grief away, 'I'd say you were a romantic, Sebastián Castellano.'

He didn't seem to notice the effort in her tone, his fingers threading through hers and drawing her close with gentle insistence. 'Apparently, there are many things you don't know about me.' He leaned forward to brush his mouth over hers. 'Perhaps a few lessons will be in order.'

The ache inside her intensified. She'd love to know more about him and not just the pain of his childhood, but about the things that brought him joy. That made him happy. That made him laugh. She wanted to know *everything*.

'And perhaps I might even like that.' She leaned into his warmth, trying to concentrate only on this moment with him and not on the fact that they'd be leaving the next day. 'I'd very much like you to teach me to ride, too.'

'Of course.' He stroked his thumb over her knuckles, a wicked glint in his eyes. 'Though you don't appear to need much teaching. You have a natural talent for it.'

Despite the ache and the tension clutched around her heart, she couldn't help smiling. 'That's the most blatant double entendre I've ever heard.'

'I could be more blatant if you like.' The wickedness in his eyes gleamed brighter, hotter, his mouth curving. 'I could even give you your first lesson here and now.'

She wanted to. Wanted to lie down with him on the hot sand and let his touch take away the knowledge of their impending departure, if only for a brief time. Wanted to keep teasing him, keep flirting with him, since being able to was new and special, and she liked it. But that would only make things worse. Deepen her longing for what she couldn't have, what he'd already told her he would never give her, and quite frankly she wasn't that much of a masochist.

'Hold that thought,' she whispered, going up on her toes to give him a quick kiss back in promise. 'For when we have a mattress instead of sand.'

'That didn't seem to bother you yesterday.'

She leaned against him, her hand on his broad chest, feeling the strong beat of his heart, relishing this peaceful moment. 'Maybe I just like saying no to you.'

Amusement lit his eyes. 'You have a natural talent for that too.'

Her chest tightened even further. She liked him teasing her in return and she couldn't resist responding to it, spreading her fingers wide to feel the heat of him through his T-shirt and the hard band of muscle beneath the fabric. 'And you like it.'

He laughed, the sound travelling through her like sunlight, turning her knees weak with want. And he lifted his free hand to push a lock of hair the wind had blown over her face behind her ear. 'I do, my lovely wife. God help me, but I do.'

Looking up into his beautiful face she almost said it, almost let slip what was in her heart. But at the last moment she bit it back. She wasn't going to ruin this night by giving him a truth he didn't want to hear, no matter how desperately she wanted to tell him how she felt.

Instead, she went up on her toes and brushed his mouth with hers. 'Good,' she whispered. 'Because I do too.'

Later, on the rooftop terrace of the villa, her hands on the pale stone of the parapet, Alice watched the rest of the sunset flaming over the ocean. The air was still warm and scented with salt and jasmine, and the turquoise of the lagoon looked as if it had been turned to flame by the setting sun, all reds and pinks and golds.

She should be enjoying the spectacle, but the ache in her chest that had begun during their evening walk had settled in. She was so tired of it. For the past few days she'd managed to push the fact that they were leaving aside, trying to exist only in the here and now, because the here and now was so wonderful. Yet as the hour of their departure loomed, she couldn't fight the pull of grief. And not, this time, for her sister or Edward, or even the baby she'd lost.

It was grief for the present that she was losing. Him, available whenever she wanted him. Ready to touch her, talk to her, hold her. Walk beside her along the sand and give her seashells. Show her some new delight in the rock pools near the beach or at her side as they snorkelled in the lagoon. His thoughtful, incisive conversation as they discussed politics and the state of the world, books and movies and everything in between over dinner. His strong arms holding her when the grief hit as it sometimes did, letting her know that she wasn't alone, that he was right there beside her.

And grief for the future that she wanted so badly and would never have.

Somehow her heart had known the moment she laid eyes on him that he was perfect for her in every way, and he was. A true soulmate. Except for the fact that he didn't feel the same way. He'd been very clear about that.

And it hurt, the thought of leaving here, of going back to their life and the reality of their marriage. He'd told her that day on the beach, when she was in his arms, that their connection was deep and emotional, that her happiness was important to him, and she'd tried to tell herself that that was enough.

But it wasn't. They'd promised to be honest with each other and yet she was terrified of telling him her deepest truth: that she was madly, passionately in love with him. Which was the one thing he didn't want. Telling him would change things between them irrevocably, because once that secret was out, she could never take it back. How it would change things, she didn't know, but she was very sure it wouldn't be for the good.

Besides, he might distance her and she'd already had that once before, and she'd hated it. She couldn't go back to it, especially now, after having these past two weeks with him. It would be like going from having everything to having nothing at all.

Still, she was tired of holding onto her secret. Tired of pretending she didn't feel it.

A footstep came from beside her and Sebastián was there, putting down a flute of champagne. He'd gone to open a bottle so they could toast their last night here.

She glanced at him and, as it always did, her breath caught. He was as gorgeous as ever in a loose white shirt and black trousers. His black hair looked as if there were threads of amber in it from the light of the setting sun, his eyes molten gold.

Her heart clenched and reflexively she looked away in case her heart was in her eyes.

'So,' Sebastián said. 'To our last night?'

Alice took a silent breath then reached for her flute and forced herself to meet his gaze. 'Our last night,' she echoed, her voice huskier than she wanted it to be, and raised her glass.

He toasted her, the glasses making a soft chiming sound as they knocked together.

She took a larger gulp of champagne than was probably wise, trying to moisten her dry throat and control the intensity of her emotions that suddenly felt choking. She wanted to leave right now, get this over and done with so she could get on with trying to figure out how to be in a marriage where she was desperately in love with her husband, while he wanted no part of that love.

'Something's wrong,' Sebastián said after a moment, watching her. 'What is it?'

Alice took another gulp of champagne, trying to resist the urge to drain her glass completely. 'Nothing.' She tore her gaze from his and stared out at the sunset. 'Sad to go home, I suppose.'

Sebastián was silent a moment. Then she felt his finger beneath her chin as he turned her face relentlessly towards him. The deep gold of his eyes held hers. 'It's more than sadness, Alice. What is it? Are you having doubts?'

His gaze was difficult to hold and she was desperate to pull away. But he'd know something was definitely wrong if she did, so she stayed where she was. 'I suppose so. Is it going to be like this when we get back home? I mean, are we going to be together like we are here back in Spain? Or are you going to put me at a distance again?'

His black brows drew down. 'No, of course I'm not going to distance you. We both decided that wasn't a good idea. The whole point of this honeymoon was to decide what kind of relationship we did want.'

'So what did we eventually decide?' She was sounding demanding and she didn't want to. She didn't want to let her doubt ruin their last evening, and yet she couldn't help it. 'I don't think we actually discussed it.'

'It's going to look like this,' Sebastian said. 'Like what we have here.'

'And what is that?' She was getting shrill now, and she hated that too.

Remind you of something?

No, it wasn't the same as her marriage to Edward. With Sebastián it would be different. He talked to her at least and he definitely wanted her. He cared for her too, that was clear. He said he would do anything to make her happy…

Anything except love you.

She could cope with that. She would have to. He'd promised her everything else so why make a drama out of it? She wasn't her sister to weep and pout if she didn't get what she wanted.

But you want more and it matters.

She hadn't thought it would, but now… Her heart twisted. Would her marriage turn into the kind of marriage she'd had with Edward? Where there was doubt and lack of communication, and one-sided uninterest?

'Isn't it obvious?' A thread of tension had entered Sebastián's voice. 'We have passion, mutual respect, interest in each other, and caring. You're important to me, Alice, you know this. I told you this. I want to make you happy. It won't be the same as before.'

She should say it was okay, that that was enough. She wanted to smile and kiss him, and make their last night a night to remember. To not ruin it by making a big song and dance about their relationship, or by pushing him into something he didn't want to give. Yet she had promised him honesty.

'I know,' she said, her voice husky. 'We do have all those things.'

His gaze turned sharp, scanning her face. 'But that's not enough, is it?'

She swallowed, her throat aching. He was too close, his scent around her, the warmth of his body a fire she wanted to warm herself against. He had become so familiar to her, so necessary...

Don't be a coward. Tell him no, it's not enough, that you want more. Tell him that what you want is his heart.

That terrified her. Every time she'd asked, she'd been refused or rejected, or simply ignored. Her parents had always prioritised Emily, and Edward had simply refused to engage. Why should Sebastián be any different?

Yet... He'd spent two weeks taking care of her, giving her pleasure, holding her when she cried and giving her little pieces of himself. He'd told her she was important to him, and he'd made her feel it too.

He was important to her. He was everything to her. She had to be honest with him. She had to. And she couldn't pretend that she was okay the way she had with Edward, the way she had with Emily and with her parents. Pretend that he didn't matter to her and that she didn't feel anything for him. Pretending was all she'd been doing for years and, yes, she was tired of it.

She didn't want to do it any more and maybe the time had come to stop.

They could have more than this if only she had the courage to ask for it.

Alice pulled away from him and took a couple of steps, putting some physical distance between them.

He frowned in puzzlement, his beautiful face lit by the setting sun, turning his hair glossy, gilding him with amber.

Her heart beat hard against her ribs. She couldn't not say it. She owed it to him and to herself. 'No, Sebastián,' she said. 'No, it isn't.'

He didn't move and yet his whole posture tensed, his face hardening. 'What more do you want?'

It was too late to back down now. She'd said the first words and now she had to say the rest of them.

Alice swallowed and lifted her chin. 'I know back in Spain I said that I didn't want love, but… I lied. I lied, Sebastián. Because that's when I realised I was in love with you.'

Something bright and intense leapt in his eyes, then it was gone. His expression hardened even more, becoming set. 'Alice. That's not what we agreed on.'

Of course he wouldn't want this. She'd known that already, but his response was proof. The small, precious hope she'd been nurturing for longer than she could remember shrivelled up and died. It was strangely freeing.

He didn't want this. He didn't want her. Which meant she could say anything she liked to him without fear of upsetting the delicate balance between them. Because it wasn't just upset, it had been destroyed.

'I know,' she said and lifted a shoulder. 'But it happened anyway.'

He stared at her, his mouth a hard line. 'This changes things. This changes everything.'

'Really?' Anger was starting to rise up inside her and she let it. 'And how, exactly, does it change things?'

He took an abrupt step forward. 'You know I can't hold you to our marriage now, don't you? You know I can't keep you.'

'Why?' Her anger leapt higher. 'Why does it make any difference at all?'

'Because I don't want love, Alice. In fact, I specifically said that our marriage would not feature love in any way.'

'So?' she flung back. 'That sounds like a you problem, Sebastián. And it certainly doesn't mean I can't love you.'

'So for how long?' he demanded, his own temper glittering in his eyes now. 'How long will this last if love is any part of it? You'll get tired of it. You'll get tired of me withholding something from you that you want. Then you'll stop wanting our marriage and you'll go behind my back with someone else.'

Hurt knifed through her. 'No,' she said furiously. 'That's *not* going to happen. How dare you think that I'd ever do something like that?'

'I thought Emily wouldn't, but she did,' he said flatly. 'Because I couldn't give her what I can't give you.'

'Couldn't or wouldn't, Sebastian?' She took a step towards him too, staring up into his furious amber gaze. 'Be clear on which it is, because that sounds awfully like a choice to me.'

He stared at her. 'Yes, you're right. It's a choice. I couldn't give her what she wanted, because I'd already given it to you.'

There was shock in her eyes, and she was staring at him as if he'd just started speaking Greek. She looked magnificent, as she always did, especially when she was in a fury. Her eyes deep and dark and full of hot temper, her hair wild and dark down her back. She wore the sexiest white dress, a halter neck that cupped her breasts and hugged her hips before swirling out into full skirts. The ends of the halter tied behind her neck and fell down her back, just begging to be pulled.

She was so beautiful and yet everything inside him was clenched tight with disappointment.

She loved him. Even though he'd told her that love could never be a part of their relationship. Even though he'd warned her. And now he could give a name to the feeling that clawed at his own heart every time he looked at her.

He loved her too. He had loved her the second he'd seen her. And he'd been telling himself lies all this time, because he'd already had a wife and he'd made promises to her. He'd wanted to be a good husband just as he'd wanted to be a good son. Telling himself that it wasn't, couldn't be love, that it was something else, something powerful and compelling and passionate, but definitely *not* love.

It was love, of course.

When he'd told himself he wasn't going to fall over that precipice, he hadn't realised he'd already fallen.

That was why it was so very disappointing. Why, even if he didn't want it to, it changed everything. Why he couldn't hold her to their marriage and wouldn't.

She'd told him it was a choice, and it was. She'd taken his heart, there was nothing he could do about that, but he could choose not to take hers in return.

'What do you mean you'd already given it to me?' Alice said softly, her anger giving way to surprise and a dawning hope.

But he couldn't allow that hope. It would be better for her if he crushed it completely, if he failed her now before he failed her at some later stage, when it would hurt her even more.

And he would fail her. He'd failed his mother, his father, and Emily, and he didn't see how it was possible not to fail Alice. Diego would take everything he had to give, and he didn't have anything left for anyone else. His son would have to come first; he had to.

She never wanted to be anyone's second choice.

No, and it killed him that she would be. But it had to be this way. With any luck, she'd understand.

'My heart, Alice,' he said roughly. 'You had it the moment I saw you and so I had nothing to give Emily.'

'What?' She'd gone pale. 'So it's my fault? Is that what you're saying?'

'No, *mi cielo*, that's not what I'm saying.' He wanted to hold her, but he couldn't allow himself that. He could never allow himself anything, that was clear. He'd thought he'd be able at least to have her in his life and at his side, but he couldn't, and he'd been selfish to think so. 'You weren't to blame for anything. As you said so eloquently, it's definitely a me problem. Because I loved you, I couldn't give Emily what she wanted, what she needed, and what I should have done was let her go. But I didn't. Selfishly, I wanted to prove that I could be a good husband, but I ended up proving the opposite.'

Mean and petty and cruel. Just like your father.

'No,' Alice breathed, the colour rushing back into her face. 'No, that's not true. You were a great—'

'I was not,' he interrupted flatly. 'Just like I wasn't a good son. My father was jealous and vindictive, and I made him worse. I got Javier fired. I didn't love Emily the way she should have been loved and ended up causing her so much pain.' His jaw ached but he made himself go on. 'Love is cruelty and pain. And everyone I love I fail. So I'm choosing now not to fail you. Do you understand?'

She was shaking her head, still staring at him in shock. 'No, Sebastian. No, I don't understand. You haven't failed anyone.' She took another step, getting close to him and he had to take a step back. He didn't want her near. She was too much of a temptation to him already and he was too weak when it came to her.

'I love you, Alice,' he said, allowing himself the luxury of saying the words once, out loud, because he would never say them again. 'But I'm not letting my heart make my choices for me, not this time. I'm going to give everything I have to Diego. Everything. He is the one person I have no choice about and he's only a baby. You will find someone else, another man who—'

'Are you serious right now?' Bright sparks of anger leapt in her eyes. 'Are you really saying that I need to turn around and look elsewhere?'

'I'm not choosing you, Alice,' he said roughly. 'That's what you always wanted. You wanted to be someone's first choice and I can't give you that. I can't give you anything but hurt and disappointment.'

'Do you really think I want to be put ahead of Diego?' Her voice was fierce, hot. 'Do you really think I'd demand that you put me ahead of my four-month-old nephew?'

'No, but I—'

'You're damn right, I wouldn't,' she interrupted furiously. 'And you're a coward for even thinking that I would. A coward for using Diego as an excuse.'

He stiffened in outrage. 'I'm not using him as an excuse!'

'Aren't you?' Abruptly she stormed up to him, her dress sweeping out behind her, all the fierce passion of her soul blazing in her eyes. 'You're using him as a reason not to even try, Sebastian. And all so you can avoid the possibility of failing.'

His own temper leapt high. 'I'm not afraid!'

'You are!' She drew herself up to her full height, magnificent as a goddess in her anger. 'You're afraid. And you're afraid because even now, even after all this time, you're still trying to make it up to your father.'

'No,' he said furiously. 'That was years ago.'

'So why are you still doing it? Why is failure the only thing you can think of when you look at me? Do you think I'm demanding? Is that it?'

'No, love is demanding, Alice.' This time he took a step, getting close to her, letting her feel his hopeless rage. 'It's vindictive and cruel and it expects everything from you. And I have nothing to give. *Nothing*.'

She didn't back away, she just stared right back at him. 'You're wrong,' she said flatly. 'It's not love that's vindictive and cruel and demanding. That was all your father. *He* was the issue, not love. And not you. Never you. I don't know why you get the two confused, but what I do know is that it's not me you're protecting, it's yourself.'

'I'm not—'

'I don't want to hear it.' The darkness of her eyes stared into his, the strength of her spirit shining through. 'I waited five years for you, and I'll be damned if I let you fall at the first hurdle, just because you're afraid. I'm also not going to leave so you can take the easy way out.' Her expression blazed with something passionate and intense. 'I love you. I loved you the day I met you. And now I've spent time with you, got to know you, I love you even more. You're the most amazing, intelligent, caring and passionate man I've ever met and what we have together is special, Sebastián. What we have is unique. I let my first marriage go without a fight, without a protest, but I'm not going to do it with you.'

She lifted a hand to his cheek, rooting him to the spot. 'I will fight for you. I will fight for what we have, because you're worth it. *We* are worth it. We *deserve* it.' Then she dropped her hand and stepped back. 'Let me know when you change your mind because I'm not leaving this place until you do.'

Then she walked right past him and off the terrace.

CHAPTER ELEVEN

ALICE STORMED DOWNSTAIRS, absolutely furious. She'd bared her heart to him, told him what she wanted, and all he'd given her in return were excuses. He had good reasons to believe them to be truths—his experience of love had been terrible, after all—yet they were excuses all the same.

He was afraid and she understood that, but she'd hoped that what they had would be greater than his fear. She'd hoped that he'd give love another chance, yet it seemed he wasn't going to overcome this.

By the time she got downstairs though, all her anger had evaporated, and as she stepped into the lounge, the tears she'd been fighting all this time finally streamed down her cheeks.

A part of her wanted to run, find the boat they'd been using and turn it out into the open sea and let it go. Let it take her far away from the island where she'd been so happy, and far away from him.

But she knew if she did that she'd be losing yet one more thing. She'd lost her baby and her marriage, her husband and Emily. She couldn't bear to lose Sebastián too, and she damn well wasn't going to.

She couldn't force him to look at himself and what he was doing, to see what she saw in him, which was a loving, generous, passionate man who'd been told nothing he could do would ever be enough to be accepted and loved. No wonder he thought love was a terrible force. No wonder he didn't want it. It must feel like mountains crushing him.

Still, she wasn't going to walk away from this. She wasn't going to accept whatever scraps he was willing to give her and she wasn't going to do what she'd done with Edward and let him withdraw from her either. She wanted to fight for him, fight for the relationship they were just starting to build, and if that meant waiting for him to be ready, to face his fear, then she'd wait.

But she wasn't leaving.

She wanted him more than she wanted her next breath and so she was going to stay here to fight for him whether he wanted her to or not.

Sebastián stood for a long time on the rooftop terrace, watching as the sun disappeared beneath the horizon. Every muscle in his body was tense and his heart felt as if it had shattered in his chest.

He couldn't give her what she wanted. He couldn't. He didn't have it in him. He had *nothing* left.

She's right. That's the excuse you use because you're afraid and you're protecting yourself.

What was wrong with wanting to protect himself, though? His father's terrible revelations had gutted him, and even though he'd tried hard afterwards to be a good son, nothing he had done had made any difference. Mateo had resented him until the end.

Could she really blame him for not wanting to open himself up to that kind of pain again? For not wanting to visit that pain on anyone else? Especially after what had happened with Emily.

When he'd married Emily, he'd been determined to be a good husband. He'd pushed aside his longing for Alice, tried to forget about her, tried to channel his passion into his wife instead of into his obsession with her sister.

But he'd failed and he'd hurt her badly enough that she'd gone looking for someone else. She'd broken her vows to him, yet he couldn't blame her. He hadn't loved her the way he should have.

He didn't love anyone the way they should be loved, because it was such an intense, powerful emotion. It caused great harm and he only had to remember Alice's white face and her dark eyes full of passion and fury to know that.

She loved him and it had brought her nothing but pain.

Yet she's still going to fight for you, for what you both could have together. Why aren't you fighting for her in return?

Why would he? When love was a never-ending grind of keeping your emotions tied down and held back, of trying to give someone enough to make them happy and failing?

The shattered edges of his heart ground against one another, pain spreading through him.

A coward, Alice had called him.

It's true. You don't want to try, because you don't want to fail. And you don't want to fail because she was right when she said you were still trying to make it up to your father. That's all you've been doing for years...

His muscles ached, everything ached. The sun was sending up its last flaring brilliance and he couldn't drag his gaze away. But he wasn't looking at it. There was only Alice standing in front of him, throwing the truth in his face, because it *was* the truth. He could see that now. That was exactly what he'd been doing and for years now, letting his father's anger and resentment colour his life. Still trying to prove himself to a man who'd died years ago.

A man who wasn't his father, he knew suddenly, because a father wouldn't do that to his son. He could see that now, because he wouldn't do that to Diego. He *loved* Diego.

And you love Alice too.

He did. And the past two weeks with her hadn't been a grind. They'd been the happiest he'd ever had and she had been happy too. Turning towards him, her face shining, smiling at him, her dark eyes full of light.

You made her happy.

Yes, he did. That was all him. And she made him happy too. Diego also made him happy. Was it as simple as that?

'It's not love that's vindictive and cruel and demanding. That was all your father...'

That was what she'd told him and...maybe she was right. Alice loved him and she'd never been cruel or petty. No, all she'd given him was happiness. So...was love happiness? Was it...acceptance?

She accepts you. She always has. She got to know you and she's still here, fighting for you. Wanting you. How can you give her nothing in return?

He couldn't give her nothing. That was it, wasn't it? That would be repeating his marriage to Emily, and he knew abruptly that the answer wasn't to walk away. Alice wasn't walking away, she was standing and fighting, and he couldn't let her be the only one. He had to fight for her too, because she deserved it. She deserved everything he could give her and that meant giving her *everything*.

His mind. His body. His heart and his soul. They were all hers.

Sebastián pushed himself away from the edge of the terrace and turned, striding down the stairs and into the living area. She wasn't there.

He went through the sliding doors and out into the front garden that sloped down to the sea and there she was, standing staring at the horizon, the last rays of the sun outlining her in gold.

'Alice,' he said quietly. *'Mi cielo.'*

Slowly she turned and their eyes met the way they had all those years ago, and he could feel it then. He let it in, fully and completely.

It was what it had always been. Love at first sight.

'What did you choose?' Her chin was still lifted and he could see that she was still prepared for a fight.

But she didn't have to fight now, not any more.

'You were right,' he said. 'When you said it was my father who was the problem, not love, you were right. These past two weeks with you have shown me what love truly is and it's…happiness, Alice. And it was you who showed me that.'

Her eyes were liquid with tears and the expression on her face put the setting sun to shame, but he went on, because nothing was going to stop him from saying the rest now. 'So, Alice Castellano, my beautiful wife. I have made my choice, and my choice is love. My choice is you. It was you five years ago and five years from now it will still be you. Those years we spent waiting were too long and I want more. I want everything. I want for ever.'

'Really?' She took a shaky breath, staring at him as if she didn't quite believe it. 'As simple as that?'

'Yes,' he said. 'As simple as that.' And then he opened his arms and she ran into them, and she was finally there, where she should have been right from the start.

In his arms.

Close to his heart.

EPILOGUE

THE HACIENDA LOOKED beautiful tonight. There were strings of lights wound all through the courtyard and the bougainvillea was magnificent. Guests filled the space, and the air was full of the buzz of conversation and the sound of classical guitar.

Alice saw him then, across the courtyard talking with Diego's new father-in-law. He was dressed in a dark suit, with a gold silk tie the colour of his eyes and, even after all these years, he was still the most beautiful thing she'd ever seen.

Apart from Diego, of course. And his new bride. And his sister, Giselle, whom they'd adopted not long after Diego and who at eighteen was growing up into the most gorgeous young woman. And of course the twins, Emily and César, whom they'd had via a surrogate, and at ten were still terrorising their poor parents. César in particular was a carbon copy of his father and he was going to break hearts one day, while Emily had decided that boys were ridiculous and she was going to be Prime Minister instead. Alice had no doubt she would be.

Their children were in the crowd somewhere, along with Diego's bride's family and a few of Alice's colleagues and Sebastián's. But mainly it was full of the children, both past and present, who'd come to the hacienda to heal.

A year after they'd got back from the island, Sebastián and Alice had decided to open their home and the stables to children from traumatic backgrounds, who could find acceptance with the horses, just as he had.

Alice considered every one of those kids her children too.

They were all here on this night to celebrate Diego's wedding, but right in this moment, Alice only had eyes for her husband.

He looked up from his conversation and their eyes met, as they'd once done long ago, and she felt it now as she'd felt it then, the thunderbolt. The lightning strike.

He was older now, with white at his temples, but the lines around his eyes and mouth were from laughter and joy. He smiled at her, then said something to Diego's father-in-law, and started towards her.

At the same time as she started towards him.

They met in the middle of the courtyard and when he held out his hand, she took it.

'*Mi cielo,*' he murmured. 'I think I've seen you somewhere before.'

'Oh, I don't think so,' she said, pretending. 'Are you sure?'

'Oh, yes.' He drew her close. 'I'm sure. In another lifetime. Or maybe many other lifetimes.'

He was so familiar to her and yet every time he touched her, the same excitement flared. She looked up at him from beneath her lashes. 'Perhaps we'll see each other in future lifetimes too?'

His smile was the whole world. 'We will. We have so much to look forward to.'

It wasn't too much of a stretch to believe him.

Theirs was a love that had been written in the stars.

It always had been.

And it always would be.

* * * * *

Were you captivated by
Spanish Marriage Solution?

Then you're bound to enjoy these
other dazzling stories
by Jackie Ashenden!

Her Vow to Be His Desert Queen
Pregnant with Her Royal Boss's Baby
His Innocent Unwrapped in Iceland
A Vow to Redeem the Greek
Enemies at the Greek Altar

Available now!